DON
QUIXOTE

DON QUIXOTE

a play by
KEITH DEWHURST

from the novel by
MIGUEL de CERVANTES

AMBER LANE PRESS

All rights whatsoever in this play are strictly reserved and application for performance, etc. should be made before rehearsal to:

London Management and Representation Ltd.
235/241 Regent Street
London W1A 2 JT

No performance may be given unless a licence has been obtained.

First published in 1982 by
Amber Lane Press Ltd.
9a, Newbridge Road
Ambergate
Derbyshire DE5 2GR

Typesetting and make-up by
Midas Publishing Services Ltd.,
Oxford

Printed in Great Britain by
Cotswold Press Ltd., Oxford

ISBN 0 906399 37 8

ACT ONE

ACT TWO

CHARACTERS

DON QUIXOTE

SANCHO PANZA
ALDONZA LORENZO
HOUSEKEEPER
PIERO PEREZ, THE CURATE
MASTER NICHOLAS, THE BARBER
NIECE
A SERVANT BOY

YANGUESAN OVERSEER
YANGUESAN CARRIER

JUAN PALOMEQUE, LANDLORD OF
  THE INN
MARITORNES
LANDLORD'S WIFE
LANDLORD'S DAUGHTER
PEDRO MARTINEZ
OFFICER OF THE HOLY
  BROTHERHOOD

FIRST SHEPHERD
SECOND SHEPHERD

HERNANDEZ

AN OFFICER
A SERGEANT
JUAN DE PIEDRAHITA (FIRST
  SLAVE)
SINGER (SECOND SLAVE)
THIRD SLAVE
FOURTH SLAVE
STUDENT (FIFTH SLAVE)
GINÉS DE PASAMONTE

TERESA PANZA

SAMSON CARRASCO

TOMAS CECIAL

DON DIEGO DE MIRANDA
A CARTER
TWO LIONS

MONTESINOS
DURANDARTE
RAGGED GIRL

PETER THE PUPPET-MAN
  (GINÉS DE PASAMONTE)
A PROPHESYING APE

THE DUKE
THE DUCHESS
DONNA RODRIGUEZ
THE STEWARD
THE CONFESSOR

BARATARIAN WOMAN
A GRAZIER
A CLERK
A PAGE

SHEPHERDESS
SHEPHERD
A YOUTH ON THE ROAD

THE KNIGHT OF THE WHITE
  MOON (SAMSON CARRASCO)
HIS SQUIRE (TOMAS CECIAL)

A DOCTOR

Puppet characters:
DON GAYFEROS
CHARLEMAGNE
MELISENDRA
A MOOR

The cast also includes: Villagers, Carters, Yanguesan Carriers, Galley Slaves, Courtiers, Dancers, Musicians, Soldiers, Guards, Shepherds, Sheep and Sheepdogs, etc.

Don Quixote was first performed at the Olivier Theatre at the National Theatre in London on 18th June, 1982, with the following cast:

DON QUIXOTE DE LA MANCHA	Paul Scofield
SANCHO PANZA	Tony Haygarth
ALDONZA LORENZO/LANDLORD'S WIFE/ BARATARIAN WOMAN	Jane Wood
THE HOUSEKEEPER/DONNA RODRIGUEZ	Edna Doré
THE CURATE/STEWARD	Derek Newark
THE BARBER/LION	Brian Glover
THE NIECE/SHEPHERDESS	Jennifer Hall
THE SERVANT BOY/STUDENT PRISONER/ SHEPHERD	Stephen Petcher
OLD PRISONER/MONTESINOS/ DOCTOR	J.G. Devlin
PAGE	Paul Davies-Prowles or Jason Smart
LANDLORD/CLERK/OFFICER	Trevor Ray
MARITORNES	Vicky Ogden
LANDLORD'S DAUGHTER/RAGGED WOMAN	Maggi-Anne Lowe
PEDRO MARTINEZ/THIRD SLAVE/ DON DIEGO DE MIRANDA	James Grant
YANGUESAN CARRIER/OFFICER OF THE HOLY BROTHERHOOD/SERGEANT	William MacBain
HERNANDEZ/BARATARIAN GRAZIER	Howard Goorney
LEADING GALLEY SLAVE	John Tams
YOUNG GALLEY SLAVE/CARTER	Roger Davidson
GINÉS DE PASAMONTE/LION/CONFESSOR	Jack Shepherd
SAMSON CARRASCO	Karl Johnson
YANGUESAN CARRIER/TOMAS CECIAL	C.J. Allen
THE DUKE/DURANDARTE	Robert Flemyng
THE DUCHESS/TERESA PANZA	Tamara Hinchco
ARCADIAN YOUTH	Martin Carthy

Other parts played by Peter Dineen, Julie Legrand, Paul Stewart and The Company.

THE BAND: John Tams (melodeon, singer), Graeme Taylor (guitar), Bill Caddick (singer), Martin Carthy (singer), Jonathan Davie (bass guitar), Howard Evans (trumpet), Michael Gregory (percussion), Steven King (synthesiser), Phil Pickett (wind instruments), Maddy Prior (singer), Linda Thompson (singer), Roger Williams (trombone).

Director	Bill Bryden
Settings	William Dudley
Costumes	Deirdre Clancy
Lighting	William Bundy
Music Director	John Tams
Fight Sequences	William Hobbs
Dances	David Busby
Music Associate	Graeme Taylor

INTRODUCTION

MIGUEL DE CERVANTES SAAVEDRA was born in 1547. His father was an unsuccessful surgeon, and the family moved continually. Cervantes lived for a time in Rome, as servant to a Spanish Cardinal, and then enlisted in the army. In 1571 he fought, and was wounded, at Lepanto, after which he served throughout the Mediterranean, until in 1575 he was recommended for promotion. He sailed for Spain but was captured by Algiers pirates, and held by them until his ransom in 1580. On his freedom he went to Madrid and tried to make his living as a writer. He had a daughter by one woman and married another, and in 1587 obtained a post as a Commissary for the Armada. He moved to Seville and became a tax-collector, but his accounts were in arrears and in 1597–98 he spent nine months in prison. The next years are obscure, until the publication in 1605 of *Don Quixote, Part One*. It swept Europe but made little money for Cervantes. He continued to write stories and plays and, in 1615, *Don Quixote, Part Two* was published. By now he was world-famous but continued to be financially embarrassed. On April 23, 1616, he died in Madrid. He left no will and was buried in an unmarked grave.

Part One of *Don Quixote* contains most of the well-known "mad" adventures such as the sheep and the windmills, and its tone is broadly comical. Its success was such that it received the ultimate flattery of a pirate sequel, to refute which was one of the motives that inspired Cervantes to write the genuine *Part Two*. This is different in tone from *Part One*. The Don and Sancho are given a curious alienation effect in that everyone they encounter recognizes them as the mythic characters of the earlier book. The mood is darker and more elegiac, and Cervantes' mind looks deeper into the ambiguities of fantasy, truth, and identity, and into the nature and value of the Don's moral impulse. When Cervantes was alive there had of course been no Knights Errant for centuries, and Spanish soldiers were engaged in bloodthirsty colonial conquests. This makes the Don's deathbed rejection of his own ideal but mad Knighthood most profoundly and mysteriously moving.

The present adaptation tries to reflect the differences between the two volumes, and to chart the Don's progress, even though I have had to cut a great deal, and have transferred the "Arcadia" scene from *Part One* to *Part Two*. The dialogue is based on the first English translation of the book, done by Thomas Shelton in 1612 and 1620.

In certain respects the text differs from that originally presented at the National Theatre. I have cut the scene in which Don Quixote meets Juan Haldudo of Quintanar, and trimmed the Galley Slaves scene. Nevertheless, this is the version which I would wish to see used in any future productions.

Finally I must express my admiration for the work of all my colleagues on the production, and especially for the performances of Paul Scofield and Tony Haygarth as the Don and Sancho Panza. They were exciting in their boldnesses, truthful in their comedy, and heartrending in their simplicity. To have seen them at all was a privilege, let alone to have watched their creations grow.

Keith Dewhurst
July 1982

ACT ONE

When we enter the theatre we see before us the high plain of La Mancha. It is vast and austere, although its warm sunshine beckons.

Gradually, the band arrive to tune up and sort themselves out. Their position reminds us of the balconies of an old house in a village that looks across the plain. When they are ready the band play the Overture, and it is a true overture, one woven out of many of the musical strands that we will hear in the play, in particular the music of Quixote's day, the bagpipes and dances of the people, the chanting of the Church, the stateliness of the Court. The Overture ends with a jolly peasant dance, and then the lights fade to black.

SCENE ONE

Of the Departure to Seek Adventures

In the darkness a cock crows, very loudly, two or three times.

Then the dawn music plays on the peasant bagpipes and drums: a tune at once simple and noble; the sun slowly rises. Against it we see the absurd silhouette of Don Quixote mounted on his horse Rosinante, his lance in his hand, his half-pasteboard helmet tied on with green ribbon.

As the sun rises higher we see Quixote's thin face and visionary eyes. He is utterly still.

Then the daylight is complete and the dawn music fades.

QUIXOTE: Fortune ordains, and reason requires, and above all, my affection desires, Sancho Panza.

> *In desperate haste a sweating Sancho Panza appears. He urges his grey, saddle-bag-festooned ass towards Quixote and stops at a respectful distance. He is out of breath. Sancho essays a smile. Quixote ignores him. Sancho sighs. Quixote barely glances at him. He is annoyed but wants to rise above it. Sancho is apologetic*

> *for his lateness, but not sure that it is safe to say so without giving further offence.*

Friend Sancho: I still cannot call to mind whether, in all the books that I have read, any Knight Errant carried his squire assishly mounted.

> *Sancho grins and shrugs apologetically.*

To which I here resolve: to accommodate you more honourably when occasion offers.

> *General gratification. Sancho squirms with pleasure.*

I care not that in the world's eye you are a poor farmer, friend Sancho, for I am Don Quixote de la Mancha and I have made you my Squire, since it was requisite and behoveful for the augmentation of my honour, and the benefit of Spain, that I myself should become a Knight Errant, and go through the world with my horse and armour to seek adventures, and practise in person what I have read in books: revenging of all kinds of injuries, and offering myself to occasions and dangers, which being once happily achieved, might gain me eternal renown.

> *A flourish from the band. Quixote strikes an even nobler pose.*

I might even be crowned Emperor of Trebizond. King of the Garimantes.

SANCHO: Sir Knight: forget not the government of the island which you promised me.

QUIXOTE: It was a custom very much used by ancient Knights Errant to make their Squires governors of the islands and kingdoms that they conquered. It may happen that I might conquer such a kingdom within six days.

SANCHO: Six days!

QUIXOTE: Do not account this to be any great matter, for things and chances do happen to such Knights adventurers as I am.

SANCHO: If by some miracle such a kingdom should befall me, should my wife Teresa become a queen?

QUIXOTE: Who doubts it?

SANCHO: I do. She's not worth a sneeze for a queen. It would agree with her better to be a countess.

QUIXOTE: Commend it to God.

SANCHO: I do, Sir.

QUIXOTE: But never abase your own mind so much as to be content with less than at least to be a Viceroy.

SANCHO: Never, Sir. I have a worthy Lord and Master who knows how to turn all to my benefit. Sir, if we are resolved to ride forth why do we tarry?

> *Quixote holds up his hand for silent patience, but offers no explanation. Sancho accepts it. He looks at the Don but there is still no response. Then the musicians start to play Dulcinea's theme as Aldonza Lorenzo, a strapping and attractive farm lass aged about twenty, appears with a bundle of flax under her arm.*

QUIXOTE: Behold! It is the Lady Dulcinea del Toboso, the princess of my captive heart!

SANCHO: It's Aldonza Lorenzo, daughter of that filthy peasant Lorenzo Corquelo.

QUIXOTE: Sweet lady, deign to remember this poor subjected heart, that for your love endures so many tortures.

> *Aldonza stops. Quixote salutes her. She ignores him and goes.*

My peerless Lady, Dulcinea del Toboso!

SANCHO: They say she's the best woman at salting pigs in all La Mancha. So they say.

QUIXOTE: Having dedicated our lance to her, we may ride forth across the ancient and famous Campo de Montiel.

> *The riding forth music strikes up — but before it or Quixote and Sancho can properly get started, a group of pursuers rushes on the stage. They are: Quixote's elderly Housekeeper; his young Niece; the village Curate, Señor Piero Perez; the Barber and Surgeon, Master Nicholas; and a Servant Boy who never says anything, although it often seems that he might.*

HOUSEKEEPER: Stop it! Stop that noise! Boy — get hold of his bridle!

> *The music dwindles. The Servant Boy grabs Rosinante's bridle.*

How dare you give the Master secret help! I suppose you think you're going with him.

SANCHO: Yes, I am.

QUIXOTE: Patience, friend Sancho. Good morrow, Niece. I cannot dwell long; you have all been enchanted, and do not understand.

> *The pursuers glance despairingly at each other. It is worse than they expected. Clearly the Curate is the one who should speak first.*

CURATE: Old friend. We beg you. Remember the last time you went on your adventures.

BARBER: You came home black and blue.

QUIXOTE: Having fought ten of the most unmeasurable and boldest giants that ever walked the earth.

CURATE: See? See? There are giants in the dance again.

HOUSEKEEPER: Giants? He fell off this ridiculous horse.

QUIXOTE: This charger is Rosinante.

BARBER: It's a decrepit bonebag.

QUIXOTE: I took four days to excogitate the name Rosinante.

SANCHO: Excogitate?

QUIXOTE: Think up.

SANCHO: Thank you.

CURATE: Master Quijana — old friend. Think of your Niece who loves you. Think what a good life you lead here.

HOUSEKEEPER: Remember my stews with more beef in them than mutton.

QUIXOTE: I am not Master Quijana. I am Don Quixote de la Mancha.

HOUSEKEEPER: Come home, Sir. There's chopped meat for your evening meal.

QUIXOTE: As I told you, Master Curate, I was rescued from the giants by my uncle, the Marquis of Mantua.

BARBER: It's the books you see: gone to his head.

CURATE: As for you, Sancho Panza, does your wife know where you are?

SANCHO: My wife, your reverence, is a most excellent woman.

HOUSEKEEPER: There you are: she doesn't know.

NIECE: It's his children I pity.

HOUSEKEEPER: Of course you do.

CURATE: What will she say when she does know?

SANCHO: If I come home with an island she'll be a countess, won't she?

CURATE: An island?

BARBER: It's delirium fugens.

CURATE: What?

BARBER: Neapolitan infectious insanity.

SANCHO: Which is why I have resolved to ride forth with my master — to defend the name of his lady.

NIECE: Lady? What lady?

> *The Servant Boy holding the bridle seems about to make a great explanation. Everybody stares at him. The Servant Boy subsides. The Curate returns to the theme.*

CURATE: What lady?

SANCHO: The lady Dulcinea del Toboso.

BARBER: Delirium fugens.

QUIXOTE: For a Knight Errant who is loveless resembles a tree that wants leaves or fruit, or a body without a soul.

NIECE: Uncle, you are not a Knight Errant.

CURATE: But you do have the life of a gentleman.

HOUSEKEEPER: Of course he does. He has lentils every Friday.

BARBER: A young pigeon on a Sunday.

CURATE: Velvet stockings for feast days.

HOUSEKEEPER: Slippers to match — and a broadcloth greatcoat.

> *The Niece points to a member of the Band.*

NIECE: Which that man is wearing!

HOUSEKEEPER: What?

> *They all stare at the Band.*

MUSICIAN: Don't stare at me, missis. It's not my fault.

HOUSEKEEPER: I'm ashamed of you.

QUIXOTE: He gave a fair price.

NIECE: Oh, Uncle. Was it not enough that you sold our land to buy books?

BARBER: It was scandalous.

QUIXOTE: I cannot ride forth without provisions.

NIECE: Why do you need to ride forth, except to go hunting as you used to do? Do not many who go for wool return again shorn themselves?

QUIXOTE: Oh, Niece. How ill you understand the matter. But that is the work of my great adversary, the enchanter Freston.

BARBER: Oh no! Not that Freston again!

> *The Curate has the notion that, persuasion having failed, they must restrain Quixote by force. His idea is to have a discussion that seems to humour Quixote under cover of which he can be encircled and dragged from his horse. This the Curate attempts to convey by his tone of voice.*

CURATE: On the other hand, though, Master Nicholas, on the other hand: I did agree with our old friend here that Palmeron of England, who dragged the evil soothsayer from his horse, was a better knight than Amadis of Gaul.

> *Everyone understands what is intended except the Barber who is too interested in the argument itself.*

BARBER: Palmeron of England?

HOUSEKEEPER: Was he a better knight than Amadis of Gaul?

BARBER: Never.

CURATE: What I am saying to you is: did not Sir Palmeron drag the evil soothsayer from his horse?

BARBER: No; and neither did the Knight of Phoebus.

> *The Curate and the Housekeeper are in despair.*

QUIXOTE: I myself have often admired most of all Sir Reynold of Mount Alban.

They all stare at him. The Servant Boy seems about to speak. The Barber stops him.

BARBER: Don't you tell your betters about chivalry! In my opinion, a nobler knight than any of them was the Knight of the Flaming Sword, who with a single backhanded stroke cut in half two malevolent dwarves.

CURATE: Master Barber: can you not understand what I'm saying to you? Did not Sir Palmeron of England drag the evil soothsayer from his horse?

At last the Barber grasps the point.

BARBER: Oh. Er — yes.

CURATE: Yes.

SANCHO: Master: I smell entanglements.

QUIXOTE: Yes. It is the work of Freston. Boy! Let go that bridle that I may ride forth!

Quixote hits the Servant Boy with his lance. The Servant Boy lets go.

The riding forth music crashes out and before anyone can prevent it, carries Quixote and Sancho away from their friends and family and across the plain.

SCENE TWO

The Dreadful and Never-Imagined Adventure of The Windmills

As Quixote and Sancho turn they see a line of windmills.

QUIXOTE: Friend Sancho: fortune addresses our affairs better than we ourselves could desire. Behold. There are now thirty or forty monstrous giants, with whom I mean to fight and deprive them all of their lives. For this is a good war, and a great service to God, to take away so bad a seed from the face of the earth.

SANCHO: Giants?

QUIXOTE: Giants.

SANCHO: What giants?

QUIXOTE: Those. There. With the long arms.

SANCHO: I pray you, Sir. Those are not giants but windmills.

QUIXOTE: They have arms two leagues long.

SANCHO: Those are their sails, that are swung about by the wind to make the mill go.

QUIXOTE: It is evident you are not au fait with the matter of adventures. Those are giants. If you are afraid, go aside and pray, whilst I enter into cruel and unequal battle with them.

SANCHO: Those are without doubt windmills.

The music begins. The sails begin to turn.

QUIXOTE: Fly not, vile creatures, for it is but one Knight that assails you!

Quixote sets himself and then charges. He disappears — then reappears, entangled with the turning sails. He is carried round. Eventually Sancho frees him and leads him away, and the music fades.

SANCHO: Sir: did I not tell you to look well at what you did? They were windmills, nor could anyone think otherwise, unless he had windmills in his brain.

QUIXOTE: Peace, Sancho. Matters of war are more subject than other things to continual change. How much more since my adversary Freston has transformed these giants into mills, to deprive me of the glory of the victory. Yet at the end, his bad arts shall but little prevail against the goodness of my sword.

SANCHO: God grant it as He may, Sir.

The Band plays a slower and more weary version of the riding forth music as Sancho helps Quixote along, both of them leading their mounts.

SCENE THREE

The Unfortunate Adventure with Certain Yanguesan Carriers

It is the heat of the day and Quixote and Sancho make their way to a meadow near a stream. Some Yanguesan Carriers have also rested nearby, with a troop of Galician mares that are in their care.

QUIXOTE: Well met, gentlemen.
YANGUESAN OVERSEER: Morning.

> *Quixote and Sancho lie down to rest.*

QUIXOTE: Sancho: did you ever see a more valorous Knight than I am, throughout the face of the earth? Did you ever read in Histories of any other that ever had more courage in assailing, more breath in persevering, more dexterity in offending, or more art in overthrowing than I?
SANCHO: The truth is that I have never read any history, for I cannot read. But what I dare wager is that I never in my life served a bolder master than you are, and I pray God that we pay not for it.

> *Silence. Quixote is bruised but won't admit it. Sancho has noticed.*

Were you not pulverated by the windmills?
QUIXOTE: Pulverized.
SANCHO: Pulverized.
QUIXOTE: If I do not complain of the grief, the reason is that Knights Errant used not to complain of any wound, although their guts did issue out thereof.
SANCHO: Speaking of guts, Master...

> *Quixote looks. Sancho takes some cheese and onions from his saddlebag.*

Belly munition.
QUIXOTE: I never found it recorded that Knights Errant did ever eat, except by chance of adventure, or in some costly

banquets that were made for them. But you begin when you please.

> *Sancho eats. One of the Yanguesan Carriers sings a song.*

What noble company is this?

SANCHO: They are Yanguesan carriers, Master, and this is a troop of mares they take south.

QUIXOTE: I think they are Knights on the way to some siege.

> *The song continues. Laziness. Siesta. Sancho is content. Eventually Quixote speaks again.*

None of these aches would matter if I had remembered to make a vial full of the balsam of Fierebras.

SANCHO: What vial is that, Master? What balsam?

QUIXOTE: It is a balsam whereof I have the recipe in memory, and which one possessing it needs not fear death, nor ought he to think that he may be killed by any wound. Therefore, after I have made it, and given it to you, you have nothing else to do but that when you see that in some battle I have been cloven in two (as many times happens) you must take fair and softly the half of my body that has fallen to the ground, and put it up again with great subtlety on the part that rests in the saddle, before the blood congeals, having evermore great care that you place it just and equally. Then give me two draughts of the balsam, and you shall see me straightway become sounder than an apple.

SANCHO: If that's true I do at once renounce the government of the island you promised and will demand nothing else in recompense of my services to you, but only the recipe of this precious liquor; an ounce thereof will be worth two reales in any place.

QUIXOTE: With less than three reales a man may make three gallons of it.

SANCHO: Three gallons!

QUIXOTE: I will do better favours yet.

> *They both settle down for a snooze. The song fades. Most of the Carriers are asleep as well. But Rosinante has*

> *sniffed the mares. He approaches them in an appropriately amorous fashion. The mares shimmy and demur. Rosinante insists. The mares become more flustered. Rosinante is most rampant. A member of the Band notices what is happening and tries to attract the attention of the Yanguesans.*

MUSICIAN: Lads. Wake up, lads.

> *No response.*

That bonebag's trying to mount your mares.

> *Finally the Yanguesan singer realizes what is happening.*

SINGER: Eh! What? Oh no! Wake up!

YANGUESAN: Eh?

YANGUESAN OVERSEER: What?

YANGUESAN: It's not an attack is it?

SINGER: It's that bonebag trying to mount your mares!

YANGUESAN OVERSEER: Well, come on! Drive him away!

> *The Yanguesans set upon Rosinante with their clubs.*

YANGUESANS: You monster! You mangy devil!

> *Rosinante is in trouble. Sancho's donkey Dapple wakens him.*

SANCHO: Uh? What? Uh?

> *Sancho looks up and sees what is happening.*

Master!

> *Quixote wakes up in time to see the Yanguesans drive poor Rosinante back.*

YANGUESAN OVERSEER: Back! Get back, you randy rattlebones!

> *Rosinante retreats. Silence. Then Quixote speaks.*

QUIXOTE: Friend Sancho: so far as I can perceive, these men are not Knights, but rascally people of vile quality. In which case you may help me to take our revenge for the outrage which they have done, before our faces, to Rosinante.

SANCHO: What revenge *should* we take, if there be so many of them and we but two: which is to say, peradventure, one and a half?

QUIXOTE: I am worth a hundred.

> *Quixote draws his sword and strikes the Yanguesan Overseer with the flat of it.*

YANGUESAN OVERSEER: Ah!

> *Seeing the man dazed, Sancho rushes in and delivers a kick.*

Oh!

> *Quixote is sublime. The Yanguesan Overseer collects himself.*

Lads. Let's see your cudgels.

> *Quixote and Sancho are utterly outnumbered.*

SANCHO: Like he says, lads, of my own nature I'm a quiet and peaceable man, and a mortal enemy of thrusting myself into stirs or quarrels.

YANGUESAN OVERSEER: This isn't a quarrel. It's a thrashing.

> *Music. Quixote and Sancho are knocked down and beaten where they lie. Then the Yanguesans go, taking their mares with them. The music stops. Silence. Sancho is the first to attempt to stir.*

SANCHO: Don Quixote! Don Quixote, Sir!

QUIXOTE: What would you have, brother Sancho?

SANCHO: I would have of your worship a draught or two of the balsam, if you have any at hand.

QUIXOTE: I do not.

> *Sancho groans. Quixote tries to get up but cannot. Slowly, Sancho lifts himself and looks at his master. Against the windmills Quixote broke his lance. Now his helmet has been utterly smashed.*

So, in one half of a day we have thrust our hands up to the very elbows in that which is called adventures.

SANCHO: Within how many days, think you, shall we be able to stir our feet?

QUIXOTE: I should not have drawn my sword against men that are not knights. The God of battles has punished me for transgressing the laws of knighthood.

> *Sancho stands up. It is painful. He is bent.*

SANCHO: Ah! Oh!

QUIXOTE: If similar rascals do us any wrong, you alone must chastise them.

SANCHO: Master: I am in more of a mood for bandages than a discourse.

QUIXOTE: Poor Rosinante. I would never have believed it of him, whom I ever held to be as chaste and peaceable a person as myself.

> *Sancho helps Quixote up.*

Oh! Ah! Oh!

> *Quixote is more or less upright. He stares into the distance.*

Sancho: I see a castle wherein I may be cured of my wounds.

SANCHO: It's an inn.

QUIXOTE: A castle.

SANCHO: An inn.

QUIXOTE: It's a castle.

SANCHO: It's a castle.

QUIXOTE: So lay me as you please athwart your beast.

> *Despite his own soreness, Sancho dumps Quixote across the saddle of his donkey, and attaches Rosinante by the halter.*

SANCHO: Well, little donkey, I have come away without ribs but you are unharmed.

QUIXOTE: Does not fortune always leave one door open in disasters, whereby to remedy them?

> *Sancho sighs and leads his sad procession on.*

SCENE FOUR

What Happened Within the Inn, which the Knight Supposed to be a Castle

It is night. There is an open fire at one end of the inn courtyard, which contains many carriers, mules and other travellers. The rooms off the arcades are lantern-lit. Shadows and flickers and illuminated faces: Velázquez.

As Sancho arrives with Quixote draped across the donkey, the landlord, Juan Palomeque the Left-handed, comes to meet them. He has a lantern.

LANDLORD: Stop there. What's this? What disease has he got?
SANCHO: No disease, Sir.
LANDLORD: Was he attacked?

> *An Officer of the Holy Brotherhood looms out of the darkness. He carries a truncheon of office.*

SANCHO: No attack, Sir. A fall from a rock, Sir. His ribs are bruised.

> *Quixote groans.*

LANDLORD: Maritornes!
MARITORNES: Coming!
LANDLORD: Maritornes!
MARITORNES: I said I'm coming!

> *Maritornes, the serving wench, arrives. She's a small, solid, buxom girl.*

LANDLORD: Hold this light and call my wife and daughter.
MARITORNES: Madam! Madam and young madam!

> *The Landlord and Sancho carry Quixote, who groans. The Landlord's wife and daughter arrive.*

WIFE: What is it? Who is he? He can't sleep here if he's diseased.
LANDLORD: He fell off a rock.
WIFE: Poor gentleman. Fetch balms and bandages.
MARITORNES: Balms and bandages!
WIFE: I said fetch them!

WIFE: My word! Was that Greek he spoke?

DAUGHTER: He's a gentleman of the other world.

> *The Landlord looks at his daughter but decides not to speak. He sighs and shakes his head.*

LANDLORD: Come away. Leave him to sleep.

> *A song begins in the courtyard. The Landlord and his family leave. Sancho lies down in the next bed to Quixote. After he has watered his mules, Pedro Martinez comes to the third bed in the room. By the time the song fades the entire inn has settled down. The fire is merely a glow. Moonlight fills the courtyard but there is very little other light. Silence — and then Maritornes, barefooted and in her smock, creeps in to seek out Martinez.*

MARITORNES: Pedro? Where are you, Pedro?

> *Maritornes gropes around the room and by mistake finds her way to Quixote, who sits bolt upright and grabs her by the wrists.*

Oooh!

QUIXOTE: Most high and beautiful lady.

MARITORNES: Ssh...!

QUIXOTE: Oh, to be able to recompense so great a favour as you have shown me.

MARITORNES: There's been a mistake made.

QUIXOTE: But I have given my faith to the unmatchable Dulcinea del Toboso, the only lady of my hidden thoughts.

> *Martinez wakes up.*

MARTINEZ: What? Who's that? Maritornes?

MARITORNES: Ssh!

MARTINEZ: Maritornes? What are you doing?

MARITORNES: He won't let me go, Pedro.

QUIXOTE: Your hair, lady, is nonetheless like wires of the glisteringest gold of Arabia.

MARTINEZ: Your jest, Sir, is an evil one.

> *Martinez gets up and hits Quixote, who releases Maritornes and cries out.*

QUIXOTE: Ah! Oh!

>*Maritornes screams. The Landlord hears and shouts out.*

LANDLORD: Maritornes? Maritornes? Is that one of your conflicts?

MARITORNES: Ssh...!

>*Sancho snores very loudly.*

MARTINEZ: This one's still asleep.

LANDLORD: Maritornes!

MARITORNES: Get back into bed.

>*They rush away from Quixote. Martinez gets into his own bed and Maritornes into that of Sancho, where she hides entirely under the clothes. The Landlord appears with a lantern.*

LANDLORD: Harlot! Where are you?

>*The Landlord peers at Quixote, who groans. The Landlord snorts in annoyance and goes to peer at Martinez. Martinez snores, loudly. The Landlord grunts and goes to look at Sancho. Sancho gently snores and whistles. The Landlord is puzzled. Then there is a sneeze from the depths of Sancho's bed. Sancho wakes up.*

SANCHO: Uh?

>*In the bed something touches him.*

Oh!

>*Sancho starts to giggle.*

Ah! Ha! Ha!

>*Under the bedclothes Maritornes starts to giggle as well.*

MARITORNES: Ooh! Aah! Ha! Ha!

>*Martinez sits up. He and the Landlord stare in horror as Sancho and Maritornes giggle and tickle each other.*

MARTINEZ: Maritornes? Where are you?

>*The Landlord indicates where she is.*

Get out of that bed!

Abruptly Maritornes appears from the bedclothes. When she sees everyone staring she starts to boo-hoo. Maritornes starts to pummel Sancho.

MARITORNES: Ooh, you little fat monster!

SANCHO: It was her doing!

LANDLORD: I'll wager it was.

The Landlord starts to belabour Maritornes.

MARTINEZ: You leave my honeysuckle alone!

Martinez wrestles with the Landlord. They all shout and struggle. The Officer of the Holy Brotherhood bursts in.

OFFICER: Stand still to the Officer of Justice, and to the Holy Brotherhood!

They are still and sheepishly silent. In the silence Quixote groans.

What's befallen you, good fellow? Have they killed you?

QUIXOTE: Is it the custom of this country, you bottle-head, to talk after so rude a manner to a Knight Errant?

OFFICER: Knight Errant?

QUIXOTE: This castle is enchanted. A giant has given me a blow to the jaw.

OFFICER: Fellow: you're out of your wits.

He turns to the others.

Enough. Stop brawling. Return to your beds.

Maritornes defiantly takes the hand of Martinez, and leads him away to her own bed. The Landlord is furious but can do nothing. He goes himself.

SANCHO: Sir, is this by any chance the vile Freston in disguise, who turns anew to torment us?

QUIXOTE: He cannot be, for necromancers suffer not themselves to be seen by anyone.

OFFICER: Are you two troublemakers — or lunatics?

SANCHO: Us? I'm a squire of renown.

QUIXOTE: Be not grieved, Sancho, for I will now compound the
precious balsam which will cure us in the twinkling of an
eye. Lieutenant: call the Constable of this fortress and have
him bring me oil of fig, wine, salt, vinegar and rosemary.
And meet me at the drawbridge.

SCENE FIVE

How Don Quixote and Sancho Left the Inn

*A cock crow and music as the sun comes up and it is a new day. Everyone
gathers round Quixote in the inn yard, to watch him drink the balsam he
has mixed.*

*Quixote drinks. There is seemingly no effect. He returns the vial to
Sancho.*

Sancho drinks. It tastes foul but goes down easily enough.

Everyone waits.

*Then the effect on Quixote is galvanic. He stiffens. He doubles up. He
straightens. He reels. He goes stiff and collapses, shivering violently.
Then suddenly he awakes and stands up, utterly refreshed.*

QUIXOTE: Friend Sancho: I am wonderfully eased, and free from
all bruising and pain.

> *Sancho cannot believe it. As yet the balsam has had no
> effect on him.*

I must depart, for all the time that I abide here is but a
depriving of the world and needful people of my favour
and assistance.

> *Quixote takes an old piece of wood that is lying about the
> yard and, using it as his lance, mounts Rosinante.*

Sir Constable: may I repay your great favours by the
revenging of you upon any miscreant that has done you
wrong?

LANDLORD: Sir Knight: all that I require is that you defray the charges whereat you have been here in the inn this night, as well as for the straw and barley given your horses.

QUIXOTE: Then this is an inn?

LANDLORD: That it is, and an honourable one.

QUIXOTE: Then I have hitherto lived in error, for in very good sooth I took it until now to be a castle. But since it is an inn, you must forgive me those expenses, for I cannot go against the customs of Knights Errant. I have never read that they paid for their lodging, or any other thing, in any inn wheresoever they lay.

LANDLORD: That concerns me nothing.

WIFE: Pay what's due, and leave these tales and knighthoods apart.

LANDLORD: I care nothing but how I might come by my own.

QUIXOTE: You are a mad Constable and a bad host.

> *Quixote spurs Rosinante and rides off. The Landlord, and everyone else, turn to Sancho, who realizes that the situation may be desperate.*

SANCHO: Being as I am, Squire to a Knight Errant, the very same rules and reason that exempt my master from payment in inns and taverns ought also to apply to me.

> *This falls upon very stony ground indeed. Sancho tries a little friendly smile. No response. Then the Landlord glances at the Carriers to see if they are in agreement with him. They are. The Landlord rips Sancho's wallet from him and then the Carriers seize Sancho's arms.*

I will not pay. I will not pay.

LANDLORD: I've taken it.

> *The Carriers roll Sancho into a blanket.*

SANCHO: No. No.

> *The Carriers toss Sancho in the blanket.*

Oh! Oh! Oh!

> *Then they roll him out and leave him lying. Everyone goes, except for Maritornes, who gives Sancho a flask.*

MARITORNES: Here: a little wine to revive you. Don't tell them I gave it to you.

> *Sancho groans. Maritornes runs away. Sancho is alone. Then his donkey comes and stands by him. No response. The donkey prods Sancho.*

SANCHO: Eh? My little Dapple. Fellow sharer in all my troubles and travels, playmate of my children, delight of my wife. Now we must go quietly to find my master, my one true friend.

> *The donkey shows its pleasure. Then Sancho sits up because the riding forth music heralds the arrival of Quixote.*

SCENE SIX

In which Don Quixote Fights Two Armies

QUIXOTE: I could not take vengeance on those persons who abused you. They were lewd and treacherous caitiffs, and not knights.

SANCHO: Master: according to my little understanding, might we not do best to return to our own village, and look to our reaping and our own goods?

QUIXOTE: Sancho: how little you know of what appertains to chivalry!

SANCHO: Master: I understand that the knights may‑ have honour, but the squires are crammed full with sorrows.

> *Quixote turns away in mock disgust before his next answer, but as he does so he is brought up short by what he sees on the horizon.*

QUIXOTE: Sancho.
SANCHO: Master?

> *Quixote indicates. Sancho looks. A column of dust is moving along the horizon.*

QUIXOTE: This day I will do such feats as shall for ever be recorded in the books of fame. That dust is caused by a mighty army, and sundry and innumerable nations which come marching there.

SANCHO: If that's so there must be two armies.

QUIXOTE: What?

> *Sancho points. There is a cloud of dust at the other side of the horizon as well.*

They have come to fight one another in the midst of this spacious plain.

SANCHO: Then what shall we two do?

QUIXOTE: What shall we do? We shall assist the needful and weaker side. There. There is the Emperor Alifamfarim, Lord of Trapobana, and there is Pentapolin, King of the Germantes. Harken to their trumpets!

SHEEP: Baaa! Baaa! Baaa!

SANCHO: I think it's sheep, Master.

QUIXOTE: Sancho: you must have conceived a fear, for one of the effects of fear is to make things appear otherwise than they are.

SHEEP: Baaa! Baaa! Baaa!

SANCHO: I can still hear a great many sheep, Master.

> *Two flocks of sheep now pour into view, bleating, with bell-necks ringing.*

QUIXOTE: Where are you, proud Alifamfarim? Come to me, for I am but one knight alone!

> *The sheep, who had been proceeding very calmly, become utterly confused and rush everywhere. The Two Shepherds are dismayed. The sheepdogs bark and scamper in vain. The music is appropriately rapid.*

FIRST SHEPHERD: Stop that madman!

SECOND SHEPHERD: Get out your sling!

QUIXOTE: Long live the valiant Pentapolin!

> *The Shepherds hurl sling-shots at Quixote and Sancho, who have to dodge and duck. Then suddenly the sheep and dogs and Shepherds are gone, and the music stops.*

All is quiet again, except for one lamb, which has been left behind and nervously sniffs the air.

LAMB: Baaa!

Quixote and Sancho turn to look at the lamb.

QUIXOTE: The malign Freston has from envy converted the enemy's squadrons into sheep.

LAMB: Baaa!

QUIXOTE: Crinklepate!

The lamb bleats and scuttles away to safety. Quixote settles his dignity and looks at Sancho. Sancho tries to look normal; then suddenly he clutches his stomach.

SANCHO: Oh! Oh! Oh!

Quixote stares at him.

SANCHO: The balsam! Oh! Oh!

Sancho, pulling down his breeches, rushes out of sight.

QUIXOTE: I believe that this evil befalls you because you are not dubbed knight.

SANCHO: [*offstage*] Oh! Oh!

QUIXOTE: It seems that the liquor does not help any who are not.

Sancho reappears. He looks shattered.

SANCHO: Why therefore did you consent that I should taste it?

QUIXOTE: Sancho: God will not fail us. Does He abandon the little flies of the air, or the wormlings of the earth, or the spawn-lings of the water?

SANCHO: You were much fitter to be a preacher than a Knight Errant.

QUIXOTE: I think we may gather that in times past the lance never dulled the pen, nor the pen the lance.

SANCHO: Master: in times past, how much did the Squires gain? Or did they agree by months, or by days, like masons' men?

QUIXOTE: They went not by the hire.

SANCHO: Oh.

QUIXOTE: They trusted to their lord's courtesy.

> *There is a rumble of thunder and a patter of rain.*
> *Sancho groans. He and Quixote hunch themselves*
> *against the weather.*

SCENE SEVEN

Of the High Adventure and Rich Winning of the Helmet of Mambrino

The shower that seemed to signify heavenly wrath against a bad squire passes in an instant, and as it does so Quixote is filled with life again.

QUIXOTE: Sancho: there is no proverb that is not true, especially that which says: where one door is shut another is opened. Am I deceived, or does there come towards us a knight on a dappled grey horse, and on his head the gold helmet of Mambrino, for which I swore the oath?

SANCHO: Oath?

QUIXOTE: That I would recover the helmet.

SANCHO: All I see is a man on a grey ass.

> *The Barber Hernandez rides on. He has put his basin on*
> *his head because of the rain. Sancho goes genially to meet*
> *him.*

Well, friend. What's this?

HERNANDEZ: What? Oh. Has the rain stopped?

SANCHO: I think so.

HERNANDEZ: I'm going to bleed a man in this small village.

SANCHO: I thought as much.

QUIXOTE: Stand aside! You! Caitiff!

HERNANDEZ: Eh?

SANCHO: It's raving chivalry.

QUIXOTE: Render me that helmet which is mine by all due reason!

HERNANDEZ: Helmet?

SANCHO: Your basin.

QUIXOTE: If not, defend yourself!

Quixote charges.

HERNANDEZ: All I want is to bleed a man!
QUIXOTE: Yield, vile pagan!
SANCHO: He wants your basin.

Hernandez jumps off his donkey for safety.

HERNANDEZ: Take it! Take it! I can bleed him in earthenware!

Hernandez flees — taking his donkey with him.

QUIXOTE: Sancho: take up the helmet.

Sancho does so.

SANCHO: You'd have to pay a reale for a basin like that.

Quixote sets it on his head. Sancho giggles.

QUIXOTE: Do you laugh, Sancho?
SANCHO: Me? No, Sir. Never.

SCENE EIGHT

Of the Liberty Don Quixote Gave to Many Wretches

A chain-gang of Galley Slaves approaches, escorted by an Officer and a Sergeant.

SERGEANT: Fall out for fresh water!

The galley slaves rush to the water and then rest.

SANCHO: This is a chain of galley slaves.
QUIXOTE: Slaves?
SANCHO: Men forced by the King to go to the galleys.
QUIXOTE: How? Men forced? Is it possible that the King will force anybody?
SANCHO: They are condemned by their offences.

QUIXOTE: So they go not willingly, where falls in justly the execution of my function: the dissolving of violences and outrages, and the succouring of the afflicted and needful.

Quixote approaches the Officer.

I pray you, Sir: inform me of the cause whereby you carry people away in this manner.

OFFICER: They are slaves condemned by His Majesty to the galleys; so ask no more for there is no more to be said.

QUIXOTE: For all that I would fain learn of every one of them in particular the cause of his disgrace.

OFFICER: Very well. We must halt for our provisions, so you may demand of them. They are men that take delight both in acting and relating knaveries.

Quixote approaches the first man, Juan de Piedrahita, who is 24 years old.

QUIXOTE: For what offence go you in so ill a guise?

JUAN: For being in love.

QUIXOTE: For that and no more? Well, if enamoured folk be cast into galleys, I might have been rowing there a good many days ago.

JUAN: My love was not such as you conjecture.

QUIXOTE: No?

JUAN: No. I loved so much a basket well-heaped with fine linen that I did embrace it so fiercely that if Justice had not taken it away from me by force I would not have forsaken it to this hour by my good will.

Quixote approaches the Second Slave, who is a downcast and melancholy person.

QUIXOTE: What is the cause of your offence?

No reply. Juan answers for the Second Slave.

JUAN: This man, Sir, goes for a canary bird; I mean, for a musician and singer.

QUIXOTE: Is it possible that musicians and singers are likewise sent to the galleys?

SINGER: Yes, Sir, for there's nothing worse than to sing in anguish.

QUIXOTE: But he who sings affrights and chases away his cares.

SINGER: Here it is quite contrary, for he that sings once weeps all his life after.

QUIXOTE: I do not understand.

OFFICER: Sir Knight, to sing in anguish is how these people say to confess upon the rack. They gave this wretch the torture and he confessed his delight — that he was a cattle thief. He is condemned to the galleys for six years, with an amen of two hundred lashes. The others despise and abuse him for confessing, and not having the courage to say no.

Quixote passes to the Third Slave.

QUIXOTE: What have you done?

THIRD SLAVE: I must mow the great meadow for ten years because I wanted ten ducats.

QUIXOTE: I will give twenty, with all my heart, to free you.

THIRD SLAVE: Then I am like one who has money in the midst of the ocean yet dies for hunger because he can get no meat to buy for it.

QUIXOTE: You are?

THIRD SLAVE: If I had in good season those twenty ducats that your lordship offers me I would have so anointed the notary's pen, and wetted my lawyer's wit, that I might today see myself still in Toledo. But God is great. I have patience.

Quixote goes to a Fourth Slave — an old man with a beard.

QUIXOTE: Why do you come here?

The old man weeps. A Fifth Slave, a Student, answers for him.

STUDENT: This honest man goes to the galleys for four years for having been apparelled in pomp, and on horseback.

QUIXOTE: Horseback?.

SANCHO: He was carried about to the shame and public view of the people.

STUDENT: You're right: and the crime for which he was condemned was for being a broker of the ear; aye, and of the body too. For in effect I mean that this gentleman goes for a bawd, and likewise for having a little smack and entrance in witchcraft.

QUIXOTE: But for that I would have compassion. For the office of a bawd is of a great discretion, and should not be practised but by people well born. As for the smack and entrance, I know very well that no sorcery in the world can move or force the will, as some ignorant persons think. For our will is a free power, and there's no herb or charm can constrain it.

> *Silence. Even the Slaves stare at him.*

OFFICER: Is your master mad?

SANCHO: Judge for yourself, Sir.

> *Quixote passes on to the Student.*

QUIXOTE: What was your fault?

STUDENT: I have jested somewhat too much with money that belonged to two cousins of mine, until no accountant could resolve it. If you, Sir Knight, carry anything to succour us poor folk, God will reward you in heaven and we will have it here on earth.

OFFICER: Beware of him. He's a great talker and a very good Latinist.

> *Quixote moves to a final man, the 30-year-old Ginés de Pasamonte, who is more heavily chained than the rest.*

QUIXOTE: Why are you more loaded with irons than the rest?

OFFICER: Because he's committed more faults alone than all the rest together, and is a more desperate knave who will try to make an escape.

QUIXOTE: What faults can be so grievous, since he has only deserved to go to the galleys?

OFFICER: He goes for ten years. He is the notorious Ginés de Pasamonte.

GINÉS: Sir, if you have anything to bestow on us give it us now and be gone, in the name of God. You tire us with your curious search of knowing other men's lives. If you would know mine I have penned it myself.

OFFICER: He says true, and leaves the book pawned in prison.

GINÉS: And likewise mean to redeem it.

QUIXOTE: Is it so good?

GINÉS: It is. It treats of true accidents.

QUIXOTE: Is it yet ended?

GINÉS: How can it be, my life being not yet ended?

QUIXOTE: Were you in the galleys before?

GINÉS: To serve God and the King I have been there another time four years. Nor does it grieve me very much to return, for there I shall have leisure to finish my book.

QUIXOTE: You seem to be ingenious.

GINÉS: And unfortunate, for mishaps do still persecute the best wits.

OFFICER: They persecute knaves.

GINÉS: I have already told you fair and softly; you were not ordered to abuse us wretches, but to guide and carry us where His Majesty commanded.

The Officer seems about to strike Ginés but Quixote intervenes.

QUIXOTE: I pray you not. It's no wonder that a man who carries his hands so tied should have his tongue somewhat free.

Quixote speaks to the Slaves.

I have gathered out of all that you have said, dear brethren, that although they punish you for your faults, the pains you go to suffer do not very well please you, and that you march towards them with a very ill will. By my order of Knighthood I know that it is one of the parts of prudence not to do by foul means what might be accomplished by fair. I will entreat these gentlemen, your guardians, they will please to loose and let you depart peaceably. There will be others to serve the King on better occasions. It seems to me a rigorous manner of proceeding, to make slaves of those whom God and nature created free.

Quixote turns to the Guards.

Good sirs of the guard. Let them answer for their sins in the other world. It is not decent that honourable men should be the executioners of other men, seeing that they cannot gain or lose much thereby. I demand this of you in a peaceable and quiet manner. If you will not do it willingly, then shall this lance and sword, guided by the invincible valour of my arm, force you to it.

OFFICER: This is a pleasant doting. Would you have us leave unto you those whom the King forces? As if we had authority to let them go, or you to command us to do it. Go on your way, Sir, and set that basin you wear on your head somewhat straighter, and search not for a cat with three feet.

QUIXOTE: You are a cat! And a rat! And a knave!

Quixote knocks the Officer down with a blow of his lance.

GINÉS: Brothers: this is the moment!

The Slaves break their chains.

SERGEANT: They've freed the chains!

Ginés seizes the Officer's pistol.

GINÉS: Run! Run! Or I'll shoot you!

The Guards run, dragging away the Officer who has had half his clothes ripped off.

SANCHO: Master. Run away. Hide in the mountains. I beg you.

QUIXOTE: All is well, Sancho, and I know what is fit to be done. Listen to me. Listen.

The Slaves listen.

It is the part of people well-born to gratify and acknowledge the benefits they receive. I desire, and it is my will, that all of you, laden with the chains from which I even now freed your necks, go to the city of Toboso, and there present yourselves before the lady Dulcinea and recount that her Knight sends you there to remember his service to her; this being done, you may after go where you please.

GINÉS: That which you demand, good Sir, is most impossible to be performed, by reason that we cannot go altogether through these ways, but alone and divided, to the end that we may not be found by the Holy Brotherhood, which will doubtlessly set out to search for us. Change this homage of the lady Dulcinea into a certain number of Ave Marias and Credos, that might be accomplished by night or by day, running or resting, in peace or in war. To ask us to return to our chains by way of Toboso is to ask for pears from the elm tree.

QUIXOTE: I swear that you, Sir whore, Don Ginesillio of Paropillio, or however you are called, shall go yourself alone with your tail between your legs and your chains on your back.

> *Ginés winks at the other Slaves. They shrug and stroll away. Then suddenly they turn and start to throw stones. Quixote goes down. The Student runs up to him and bangs him on the head with his own basin.*

GINÉS: Take his doublet!

> *Quixote loses his doublet and Sancho his waistcoat. Ginés rides off on Sancho's donkey. Then everyone has gone and Quixote and Sancho are alone.*

QUIXOTE: I have oft times heard it said that to do good to men unthankful is to cast water into the sea. I met some mournful, miserable wretches strung together like beads on a rosary and did for them what my duty requires. The rest is no affair of mine. So have patience, Sancho, and be wiser next time.

SANCHO: Me! You will take warning by this as much as I am a Turk. But if you do believe me for once, you can escape a greater grief. The Holy Brotherhood cares not two beans for all the Knights Errant in the world. They will presently issue forth in troops to search for us and the galley slaves.

QUIXOTE: You are a natural coward.

SANCHO: Over there is the Sierra Morena. We must depart and imbosk ourselves.

QUIXOTE: Upon a condition.

SANCHO: A condition?

QUIXOTE: You will never tell alive or dying to any mortal creature that I withdrew myself for fear — but only to satisfy your requests.

SCENE NINE

Which Treats of the Penance that the Knight Did in the Sierra Morena, in Imitation of Beltinebros

QUIXOTE: Being in this thickest and roughest part of the mountain I have in my mind to achieve a certain adventure by which I shall seal all that which may render a Knight Errant complete and famous.

SANCHO: Is the adventure very dangerous?

QUIXOTE: No. But all consists in your diligence.

SANCHO: In mine?

QUIXOTE: Yes; for if you return speedily my pain will also end shortly.

SANCHO: Return?

QUIXOTE: From Toboso, and my lady Dulcinea.

SANCHO: What do you mean to do?

QUIXOTE: A penance, in imitation of Beltinebros, who was disdained by his lady.

SANCHO: Has the lady Dulcinea disdained you?

QUIXOTE: Never.

SANCHO: Then what's the reason for this penance? What occasion has been offered to you to become mad?

QUIXOTE: None. But there is the point, and therein consists the perfection of my affairs. A Knight Errant who runs mad on any just occasion deserves neither praise nor thanks. The wit is in waxing mad without cause, whereby men may wonder that if dry I could do this, what would I have done being watered? I am mad, and will be mad, until you return with my lady's answer. If it be such as my loyalty deserves, my madness and penance shall end.

SANCHO: What if it is not such?

QUIXOTE: I shall die. But now I must tear my apparel, throw away my armour, and beat my head about these rocks — with many other things of that kind that will strike you into admiration.

SANCHO: Sir, I beseech you. See well how you give yourself those knocks with rocks. Can you not content yourself with striking your head on water?

QUIXOTE: Take care with my lady. Her father, Lorenzo Corquelo, has brought her up closely.

SANCHO: Aldonza Lorenzo can throw an iron bar as well as the strongest lad in the parish. She may, at the very time of my arrival, be combing flax, or salting a pig, whereat I would be ashamed and she somewhat displeased. Besides, pondering well the matter, I cannot conceive why Aldonza Lorenzo should care whether I or a chain of freed galley slaves go and kneel before her.

QUIXOTE: You are too great a prattler. Do you think, Sancho, that the poets who celebrated certain ladies at pleasure all had mistresses? Were the Silvias and suchlike, wherewith all the books, ditties, barber's shops and theatres are filled, truly ladies of flesh and bone?

> *Sancho shrugs.*

They were for the greater part feigned, to serve as a subject for their verses. And thus it's also sufficient for me to believe and think that the good Aldonza Lorenzo is fair and honest. I make account of her as the greatest princess in the world. She has beauty and a good name and I imagine her in my fantasy to be as well in principality, and let every man say what he pleases.

SANCHO: Master: you have great reason and I am an ass. Farewell.

QUIXOTE: I would have you wait, Sancho, at least to see me stark naked, playing a dozen or two raving tricks, for I will despatch them in less than a half hour.

SANCHO: I entreat you, Sir, that I may not see you naked, for it will turn my stomach.

QUIXOTE: Stay, Sancho; I will do it in the space of a Creed.

> *Quixote gives two or three jerks in the air and then bounces completely offstage.*

SANCHO: Come back, Sir! I'm satisfied! Sir! I am now satisfied that I can swear that you are mad.

SCENE TEN

How the Curate and the Barber Put their Design into Practice

Night falls and the stage once again becomes the inn. This time the Curate and the Barber, Master Nicholas, are among the travellers.

Sancho appears, leading Rosinante.

BARBER: Master Curate, is not that short-legged person who approaches Sancho Panza, that left with our adventurer to be his squire?

CURATE: It is; and that is our Don Quixote's horse.

> *The Curate calls out.*

Friend Sancho Panza: where is your Master, whom we intend to recover?

SANCHO: Sir Curate? Master Nicholas? I can't tell you.

BARBER: Why not? Have you slain him?

SANCHO: Every man is slain by his destiny, or by God that made him.

BARBER: Get us that horse's owner, or stand to your answer.

SANCHO: I will. I will.

CURATE: Recount your adventures, from the beginning to this present end.

SANCHO: Well...

> *Sancho has no chance. He takes a deep breath and plunges. As he does so there is music and a dance, so that we do not hear him but can guess from his gestures and*

> *their reactions what adventure he is describing. When the dance stops there is an awestruck silence.*

BARBER: Sancho: I am newly amazed.

CURATE: Will you not dine with us?

SANCHO: No, because this is the inn where I was rolled in a blanket and I distrust it; and I must go to Toboso, to my lady Dulcinea.

> *Sancho goes.*

CURATE: Just fancy the vehemence of Don Quixote's frenzy.

BARBER: It's carried away his judgement.

CURATE: But why labour to dispossess him of the error, if it hurts not his conscience?

BARBER: True.

CURATE: Spoken like a discreet man, and with understanding of the duty of a Christian.

BARBER: We must still devise how to carry him back to our village.

CURATE: Is not everything in Don Quixote's head made by way of enchantment?

BARBER: Good idea.

CURATE: We will enchant him back to La Mancha.

SCENE ELEVEN

The Artificial Manner Used to Dissuade the Knight from Continuing his Penance

Next day in the Sierra Morena. Quixote, naked to his shirt, lean, yellow and almost dead from hunger, wanders, singing, across the mountainside. When the little song is finished Sancho makes a cautious approach.

SANCHO: Master? How are you, Sir?

QUIXOTE: Swallowed, friend Sancho, in the gulfs of sorrow and versifying. What said my lady?

SANCHO: She commanded you to repair at once to Toboso.

QUIXOTE: Never: until I have done feats worthy of her gracious favour.

SANCHO: Sir, you look faint with hunger and in danger thereby never to become an Emperor.

> *The Barber and the Curate enter. The Barber is mounted. They have cloaks. A cage is brought on with them.*

QUIXOTE: What procession is this, and what do they seek among these thoroughfares?

CURATE: Knight, we are enchanters come to carry you to Ethiopia, where your penance may be more speedily and perfectly achieved.

QUIXOTE: Enchanters? Ethiopia?

CURATE: Will you enter the imperial carriage?

SANCHO: Master: it's a cage.

CURATE: Cease, Squire, that we may assist the worthy Knight.

> *Quixote is helped into the cage.*

SANCHO: Master: it's a cage!

QUIXOTE: I have never, in many and very grave histories of Knights Errant, read that they were encaged. It drives me into a great amazement, but perhaps most chivalry and the enchantments of these our times follow a course different from those of former ages. And peradventure it may be also that as I am a new Knight in the world, so they have invented new enchantments. What do you think, Sancho?

SANCHO: Sir: I think that the truth is that you are as enchanted as my donkey who is missing. Your judgement is whole and sound. You eat and drink and do your necessities as other men do. Master Curate. Master Curate — I know you. I know you, Master Nicholas. Cover your face never so much I understand your meaning.

BARBER: Snuff the candles! Are you of your master's confraternity?

CURATE: Will you keep him company in the cage?

SANCHO: Sir: this is the Curate of our village, and the Barber, and the plotters of your carrying away.

QUIXOTE: Sancho: it may well befall that these men seem to be such. But that they are so really I would not have you believe in any manner. Those which enchanted me have assumed their semblance and likeness.

SANCHO: Our Lady assist me! Are you so brainsick?

CURATE: He is, as you well know.

The cage sets off. The Inn People come out.

WIFE: Poor soul! Poor old man!

QUIXOTE: Good ladies: do not weep, for those mischances are incident to those who profess as I do.

CURATE: Get on!

The riding forth music crashes out as the cage and the little procession cross the Plain of La Mancha.

SCENE TWELVE

Of How They Entered Don Quixote's Village At about Noon on a Sunday

The Villagers are in the square. There is excitement and curiosity. The music stops.

HOUSEKEEPER: It's the Master! It's Master Quijana back again!

Quixote's Niece and the Servant Boy come out to look for him.

NIECE: Uncle? Where is he? Uncle?

The Servant Boy has found Quixote and helped him down from the cage. He seems about to call the Niece and so speak at last but is too moved by Quixote's condition to do so. Quixote stares round. He sees his Niece.

QUIXOTE: Uncle?

NIECE: Do you not know me?

QUIXOTE: Where am I? Are we all together in Ethiopia?

NIECE: We are at home, Uncle, where you will stay, in sight of our own good fields.

CURATE: Aye. Cherish him carefully.

> *Quixote is led indoors and the cage is removed. Sancho is alone. Then Dapple comes on.*

SANCHO: Dapple, my little donkey, you've found your way home.

> *Teresa Panza runs on.*

TERESA: Husband Sancho.

SANCHO: Teresa my wife.

TERESA: Well, what profit have you reaped? What petticoat have you brought me? What shoes for the little boy?

SANCHO: None of these things, good wife, but other things of more moment and estimation.

TERESA: What can be bought with your things of great moment and estimation?

SANCHO: Nothing.

> *Teresa sighs and shakes her head. She opens her mouth to speak but Sancho checks her.*

But if it pleased God that Don Quixote should travel again to seek adventures, you will see me the Governor of an island.

> *The music is perkily triumphant. Sancho offers Teresa his arm, bows to the audience and off they go.*

END OF ACT ONE

ACT TWO

A reprise of parts of the overture brings back the audience. Village characters slowly drift on and we begin.

SCENE ONE

The Discourse that Passed Between Don Quixote, Sancho, and the Bachelor Samson Carrasco

The music becomes a song sung by the Women as they do their washing at the communal washing-place. Among the Women are Quixote's House-keeper, Teresa Panza, and Aldonza Lorenzo.

The washing-place is near Quixote's house and, helped by his Niece, he comes out to sit in the sun. He has a green baize waistcoat and a red toledo bonnet. The Niece sits nearby with her sewing.

According to Part Two of the book a month has passed since Don Quixote's return in the cage, although in real time Part Two was published ten years after Part One. Perhaps the wisest thing to say is that some time has passed, and Don Quixote does seem older and more frail.

The Barber has also come outdoors, and is shaving the Curate. It is all a gently pleasant outdoor village scene. When the washing has been pounded some of it is hung out to dry, and the Women drift away.

Aldonza looks back at Quixote. She's still amused by him.

QUIXOTE: Who's that?
NIECE: Who?
QUIXOTE: There.
NIECE: Oh, that's Aldonza Lorenzo from up the road — Toboso.
QUIXOTE: So it is.

> *Aldonza goes. The Barber and the Curate have heard what Quixote said and are satisfied. They think that he is cured and that it is safe to say so openly to the Niece.*

CURATE: Well, lady. It gives us great joy to see that our old friend continually gives signs of being in his right judgement.

BARBER: It does. Great joy.

NIECE: And to us, Master Nicholas.

> *The Housekeeper comments as she hangs out her washing.*

HOUSEKEEPER: It's the comforting meats I give him.

CURATE: Good morrow, old friend.

QUIXOTE: Good morrow.

NIECE: We thank God, do we not Uncle, for your good understanding.

QUIXOTE: We do. We thank God.

BARBER: May we sit with you, old friend?

QUIXOTE: You are most welcome.

CURATE: [*sotto voce to the Barber*] Do not touch upon any point of Knight Errantry.

BARBER: Not one.

> *The Barber and the Curate sit with Quixote. The Barber clears his throat. Silence. Then he opens what he regards as a safe conversation about the events of the day.*

The Turks have come down with a powerful army — so they say.

NIECE: Indeed?

BARBER: His Majesty has made strong the coasts of Naples, Sicily and Malta.

CURATE: Most politic.

QUIXOTE: If my counsel might prevail, I would advise His Majesty to use a prevention that he is far from thinking on at present.

BARBER: What would that be?

QUIXOTE: I would not tell it here now that it should be early tomorrow in the ears of some Privy Councillor, and that another should reap the praise and reward of my labour.

BARBER: For me, I pass my word here and before God, to tell neither King nor Kaiser nor any earthly man what you say.

QUIXOTE: Your word is good, because I know you to be honest.

CURATE: If he were not, I would make it good, and undertake for him that he should be dumb in the business.

QUIXOTE: And who shall undertake for you, Master Curate?

CURATE: My profession — which is to keep counsel.

> *Quixote nods. He looks round, to be sure that no one else is within earshot, and then speaks confidentially.*

QUIXOTE: Body of me, is there any more to be done then, but that the King cause proclamations to be made, that at a prefixed day, all the Knights Errant that rove up and down Spain repair to the Court?

CURATE: Knights Errant?

BARBER: Hang me!

NIECE: What? Has he a disease to turn Knight Errant again?

CURATE: I believe him to be sensible enough. All is fiction, as your Uncle knows: dreams, set down by men waking or, to say trulier, by men half asleep.

QUIXOTE: There's another error into which many have fallen, who believe not there have been such Knights in the world.

> *They are aghast at Quixote's intractability. Unfortunately this is the very moment at which Sancho chooses to appear, in the hope of catching a word with Quixote.*

NIECE: There. There is the very proof of my Uncle's disease.

HOUSEKEEPER: What do you want, you blood-hound?

NIECE: Get to your own house.

HOUSEKEEPER: You are he and no one else who ring-leads my master and carries him astray.

SANCHO: Woman, I am he that is distracted, ring-led and carried astray by your master, who promised me an island that I yet hope for.

NIECE: A plague on your islands. Get home and govern there.

HOUSEKEEPER: You bundle of mischief.

NIECE: Sow your grain, and forget islands.

> *Sancho ducks away out of sight.*

QUIXOTE: Friend Sancho? Was that friend Sancho?

NIECE: No, it was not.

QUIXOTE: It was!

NIECE: Did I not hear you say, gentlemen, that you were to dine together?

CURATE: Ah. So we are.

BARBER: What?

> *The Curate jerks his head: time to take the hint and go.*

Oh. Of a certainty. Smoked codfish.

CURATE: Farewell, old friend.

QUIXOTE: If His Majesty were well served, it might save a great deal of expense.

CURATE: And the Turk might go shake his ears.

> *The Barber and Curate mutter to themselves on their way home.*

I despair of his recovery.

BARBER: He's besotted with his damned Knights Errant. Will he take flight again, do you think?

CURATE: No doubt.

BARBER: I wonder not so much at the Knight's madness, as at the Squire's simplicity, that believes in these islands.

CURATE: God mend them both.

> *They go off, very perturbed.*

QUIXOTE: Nonetheless, niece: I would speak with my friend Sancho.

NIECE: Uncle, why go on blindly? Why have us think you are valiant when you are old, that you are strong when you are sickly, and that you are able to make crooked things straight, when you are yourself crooked with age?

QUIXOTE: Niece, fortune ordains, and reason requires, and above all, my affection desires, Sancho!

NIECE: God help me!

> *The Niece goes off. Sancho reappears. He beckons. Samson Carrasco appears. A 24-year-old man of the village who has just returned from University.*

QUIXOTE: What? Samson Carrasco?

SAMSON: The same, Sir.

SANCHO: Home from study in Salamanca.

QUIXOTE: Are you now a Bachelor?

SAMSON: I am, Sir.

SANCHO: He has news to which all that was said hitherto is but cakes and white bread.

QUIXOTE: News?

SAMSON: Sir, your History is in print, under the title of "The Most Ingenious Gentleman Don Quixote de la Mancha".

QUIXOTE: Ingenious?

SAMSON: Ingenious.

SANCHO: I am mentioned too, as one of the chief parsonages.

QUIXOTE: Parsonages?

SAMSON: Personages — and Dulcinea del Toboso is in it too, and all matters that passed between you.

QUIXOTE: In what estimation am I held?

SAMSON: By the common people — as a notable madman. Yet the book prints in Madrid, in Portugal, in Barcelona, Valencia, Antwerp and London.

QUIXOTE: Where the enchanters, it is said, have a wondrous power over the rainfall.

SANCHO: But how could the historian that wrote our adventures have knowledge of them?

QUIXOTE: Assuredly, he is a sage enchanter.

SAMSON: He is a Moor, named Cid Hamate Berengena.

QUIXOTE: A Moor!

SAMSON: He has painted your gallantry and great courage to the life.

QUIXOTE: That should content a man, to see himself living, to have a good name from everybody's mouth, and to be printed in the press. With a good name, I say, for otherwise, no death could be equalled to that life.

SANCHO: What does the author say of me?

SAMSON: That you were too credulous to believe that your government of the island might be true.

QUIXOTE: There is sunshine yet upon the walls, and when Sancho comes to be of more years with the experience of them, he will be more able and fit to be a governor.

SANCHO: Hang me! But am I called a coxcomb?

QUIXOTE: Sancho, interrupt not the Bachelor, whom I desire to tell me which of the exploits of mine are most ponderous in this history.

SAMSON: Some delight in the adventure of the windmills.

QUIXOTE: The windmills?

SANCHO: He means the giants.

SAMSON: Others in the description of the two armies that were flocks of sheep; others again say that the freeing of the galley slaves goes beyond them all; and some would be glad if the author had omitted some of the infinite bastings that were given Sancho and Don Quixote.

SANCHO: Aye. There comes the truth of the story!

QUIXOTE: Actions that neither change nor alter the truth of the story are best left out, if they redound to the misprizing of the chief person of the history.

SAMSON: Yet you are known by all sorts of people, so that they scarce see a lean horse pass by but they say, "There goes Rosinante".

QUIXOTE: Does the author promise a second part?

SAMSON: He does.

QUIXOTE: For that we must make another sally.

SANCHO: I know that if you took my counsel we should be abroad now, remedying grievances, and rectifying wrongs as good Knights Errant are wont to do.

QUIXOTE: All this is most auspicious.

> *Silence. Then they realize the significance of what Quixote has said. Sancho seems about to explode with pleasure. Quixote checks him.*

Sssh!

> *Quixote whispers.*

We will depart in three days.

> *Again Sancho wants to explode.*

Sssh!

Sancho settles down. Quixote still whispers.

Which way, in your opinion, should I begin the journey?

SAMSON: [*matching the sotto voce*] You should go to the city of Saragossa, where the solemn jousts are held.

SANCHO: [*whispering*] Capital!

SAMSON: [*still sotto voce*] But guard well your life, for it belongs not to you, but to those you must assist.

> *Sancho nods vigorously and is about to speak but then tries to look innocent because the Niece has stopped outside and is glaring at them. Quixote clears his throat and attempts to speak normally.*

QUIXOTE: Master Bachelor, will you not take a pittance with us, and describe to my niece how the author of the History has spoken of me?

> *Quixote and Samson Carrasco go indoors. The Niece glares again at Sancho and then goes in herself. Sancho rubs his hands and then goes into a gleeful imitation and remembrance of one of Quixote's fantastical salutes. He checks himself when he realizes that his wife Teresa is watching him.*

TERESA: What's the matter with you that you are so joyful?

SANCHO: Teresa: I am determined to serve my master Don Quixote once more.

> *Teresa is not pleased.*

My poverty will have it so.

> *Teresa sulks.*

Yet I am sad again, to leave you and my children. If it pleased God that I might live quietly at home without putting myself in these deserts and crossways my content might be more firm.

TERESA: Sancho: ever since you've been a member of a Knight Errant you've talked so round-about the bush that nobody can understand you.

SANCHO: Let me tell you that if I thought not before long to be the governor of an island I should die suddenly.

TERESA: Love you, you fool! You were born without a government, you have lived without a government, and without a government you must go or be carried to your grave, when it shall please God.

SANCHO: Peace!

TERESA: How many be there in the world that live without a government, yet they live well enough and well esteemed of?

SANCHO: You shall become a countess!

TERESA: I don't want to be a countess!

SANCHO: You must be!

> *Teresa starts to cry.*

Sssh! Very well! Sssh! I shall defer it as long as I can.

> *Teresa seems content.*

Now must we go home and tell the dappled grey donkey the news.

> *As Sancho and Teresa go off, Samson Carrasco reappears from Quixote's house. He sighs deeply and shakes his head. The Curate and the Barber return. They have been waiting to speak to Samson ever since, earlier in the day, he told them about the book of Quixote's adventures.*

CURATE: Well? What do you think? Is it as bad as we feared?

SAMSON: It is.

CURATE: Can Don Quixote be persuaded to stay at home peaceably?

SAMSON: No.

BARBER: I knew it.

CURATE: Will he trouble himself with his unlucky adventures?

SAMSON: Yes. It's impossible to stay him.

BARBER: What's to be done?

> *Samson whistles. Tomas Cecial, a peasant of the village, comes on.*

SAMSON: This is Tomas Cecial, Sancho Panza's neighbour, a merry knave and a witty.

CURATE: Yes. We know. What's to be done?

SAMSON: I should meet with Don Quixote upon the way, like a Knight Errant, and fight with him. To overcome him will not be difficult, and there should be a covenant agreement, that the vanquished should stand to the courtesy of the vanquisher.

CURATE: So?

SAMSON: So that Don Quixote, being vanquished, I should command him to get home to his town and house, and not to stir from there in two years after, until I should command him to the contrary. So that in this time of requesting he might forget all his vanities, or we might find some convenient remedy for his madness. So — Tomas Cecial, will you be my Squire?

CECIAL: I will, Sir.

BARBER: How will you disguise yourself?

CECIAL: I'll put on a false nose.

BARBER: Perfect.

CURATE: Things are easily conceived, and enterprises easily undertaken, but very hardly performed.

SAMSON: Master Curate, I will soundly bang Don Quixote, and restore him to his wits!

SCENE TWO

The Prosperous Accomplishment of the Adventure of the Lions

Music, tremendously flourishing and triumphant, heralds the entrance at one side of Quixote and Sancho, and at the other of Don Diego de Miranda, the man in the green coat.

DON DIEGO: Are you Don Quixote de la Mancha, otherwise called the Knight of the Sorrowful Countenance, who has merited the honour of being imprinted in almost all the nations of the world, and thirty thousand more of these volumes are likely to be printed, if heaven prevent not?

QUIXOTE: Although one should not praise himself, yet I must needs do it, there being none present that may do it for me.

DON DIEGO: Yet is it possible that in this day there be Knights Errant in the world? Is what is written in your History true?

QUIXOTE: Who are you, Sir, since you have had imparted to you my condition and life?

DON DIEGO: My name is Don Diego de Miranda. I spend my life with my wife and children and friends. I search not into other men's lives, nor am I a lynx to other men's actions. I hear every day a Mass, and give goods to the poor, but without making a muster of my good deeds, so that I may not give way to hypocrisy. I am devoted to our Blessed Lady, and always trust in God's infinite mercy.

SANCHO: Your worship is the first saint that in all the days of my life I ever saw on horseback.

DON DIEGO: I am no saint but a great sinner.

QUIXOTE: How many sons have you?

DON DIEGO: One — who is not so good as I would have him. He is about eighteen years of age and mad upon poesy.

QUIXOTE: Children, Sir, are pieces of the very entrails of their parents, so let them be good or bad, they must love them as we must love our spirits that gave us life.

> *Trumpets. A cart approaches, with two lions and a guard.*

Whither go you, my masters? What cart is this?

CARTER: The cart is mine. The carriage is two fierce lions, caged up, which the General at Oran sends His Majesty at court, for a present.

QUIXOTE: Are the lions big?

CARTER: So big that there never came bigger out of Africa. They are hungry, and therefore I pray you, Sir, give us way. For we need to come quickly to where we may feed them.

QUIXOTE: Give way? I vow to God, your General who sent them shall know whether I be one that am afraid of lions. Open the cage, honest fellow. Let your beasts forth, for I'll make them know in the midst of this plain who Don Quixote is, in spite of those enchanters that sent them.

SANCHO: For God's love handle the matter so that my master meddles not with these lions. For if he does they'll worry us all.

DON DIEGO: Is your master so mad that he will fight with wild beasts?

SANCHO: He is not mad, but hardy.

DON DIEGO: I will make him otherwise.

QUIXOTE: Open the cage. Hasten.

DON DIEGO: Sir, has not valour grounded on rashness more madness than fortitude? These lions come not to assail you. They are carried to be presented to His Majesty.

QUIXOTE: Pray get you gone, gentle Sir, and deal with your tame partridge and your murdering ferret, and leave every man to his function. This is mine, and I am sufficient to know whether these lions come against me or not.

Quixote turns to the Carter.

Good man slave, open the cage, or I will nail you with my lance to the cart.

CARTER: Bear witness my masters: I am forced against my will to open the cage and let loose the lions.

DON DIEGO: Do not attempt this madness.

QUIXOTE: I know what I do.

SANCHO: I beseech you to desist. Compared to this the windmills were cakebread. I've looked through the bars. That lion is as big as a mountain.

QUIXOTE: Your fear will make him as big as half the world. Get out of the way and leave. If I die in the place you know our agreement. Repair to Dulcinea, and that's enough.

DON DIEGO: He is truly a madman!

Don Diego and Sancho scatter.

QUIXOTE: Fellow. Make haste. Should I fight on horse or foot? On foot, I think, commending myself to God and Dulcinea.

Quixote dismounts.

Open the cage!

CARTER: On your own head be it.

> *The Carter opens the cage and runs away. Quixote assumes a warlike posture. The Big Lion sticks its head out, looks around, washes its face and yawns.*

QUIXOTE: Leap out, that I might grapple and slice you in pieces.

> *Both Lions yawn and lie down.*

Fellow: give them two or three blows to make them come forth.

CARTER: No: for if I urge them I shall be the first that they tear to pieces.

QUIXOTE: I shall defend you.

CARTER: Sir: be contented. They might have come out if they would. No brave combatant is tied to more than you have done: shown your courage, defied your enemy, and expected him in the field.

QUIXOTE: True. True it is, friend. Shut the door, and give me a certificate in the best form that you can, of what you have seen me do here.

> *The Carter shuts the cage.*

CARTER: All clear! Come out now! All clear!

> *Sancho and Don Diego reappear.*

SANCHO: Hang me. My master has vanquished the wild beasts.

QUIXOTE: What think you of this, Sancho? Can enchantment now prevail against true valour?

> *Quixote turns to the Carter.*

Fellow, if His Majesty chance to ask who did it, tell him the Knight, not of the Sorrowful Countenance, but of the Lions; for henceforward I will that my name be changed, and in this I follow the ancient use of Knights Errant, that would change their names when they pleased, or thought convenient.

> *Trumpets. The Lion's cage is driven off.*

DON DIEGO: Sir: are you a wise madman, or a madman that comes somewhat near a wise man?

QUIXOTE: I am not so mad or shallow as I seem, for valour is a virtue betwixt two extremes, and it is less dangerous for him that is valiant to rise to a point of rashness than to fall or touch upon the coward.

DON DIEGO: What confounds me is that all that you have said and done is levelled out by such lines of reason.

QUIXOTE: It is; and now Sir, since it is not fit that Knights Errant should be too long idle, you must show me where on my road I might find Montesinos' Cave, of which there are so many terrifying tales in every man's mouth.

SCENE THREE

Of Montesinos' Profound Cave, whose Strangeness and Impossibility Make this Adventure to be Held for Apocrypha

In the shaft of light from the cave's only opening, in the roof, we see Quixote descending at the end of a rope. As his feet touch the bottom he is amazed by what he sees.

QUIXOTE: Sancho: there is a fair and delightful meadow. There is a castle, a royal and sumptuous palace whose walls and battlements appear to be of clear transparent crystal.

Montesinos appears.

MONTESINOS: It is long since, renowned Knight Don Quixote de la Mancha, that we who live in these enchanted deserts have hoped to see you, that you might let the world know what is contained here.

A Knight and a Ragged Girl appear.

KNIGHT: Don Quixote de la Mancha. I am Durandarte, once the flower and mirror of all lovers and valiant knights, but now I am wretched for my great heart has been from my bosom torn. But I tell you who have revived the ancient art of chivalry which is now forgotten. Through your meditation and valour I may perhaps become disenchanted and do great deeds. Don Quixote I say, shuffle the cards.

RAGGED GIRL: Your worship, I am in great want and beg of your worship most earnestly but six reales for the purchase of a cotton dress or as many as you have about you.

The Knight and the Ragged Girl disappear.

DON QUIXOTE: Is it possible, Sir Montesinos, for people even when enchanted to be in want?

MONTESINOS: Believe me, Don Quixote de la Mancha, want is everywhere, it extends to all regions, reaches all people and does not even spare the enchanted.

Don Quixote recognizes his family in wedding array coming towards him.

DON QUIXOTE: Master Curate? Master Nicholas? Niece, my own serving lad. Friends! Old friends!

MONTESINOS: Enchanted, Sir Knight. All enchanted.

The wedding disappears. A group of people occupy the stage: gunshot and they freeze. It is Goya's famous execution painting. The stage fills with people. They are running and screaming. They freeze when Aldonza Lorenzo is centre stage. It is Guernica.

DON QUIXOTE: Dulcinea! My lady Dulcinea!

We hear the noise of the Stukkas.

What? What beasts are these? What dragons? I will defend you.

The Stukkas get louder. Machine-gun bullets rip across the stage. The people run and die. Except for Aldonza.

A song is heard: single voice.

The scene changes as the flag arrives and the company march through the auditorium.

Quixote and Sancho are alone in the fresh air.

How long was I down there?

SANCHO: A little more than an hour.

QUIXOTE: That cannot be.

SANCHO: God take me if I believe a word of all this you have spoken.

QUIXOTE: They were enchanted. Now indeed I positively know that the pleasures of this life pass like a shadow and a dream and wither like flowers of the field.

> *Sancho demurs.*

Why do all things that are difficult seem to you to be impossible?

SANCHO: Master: for the love of God have a care of yourself.

SCENE FOUR

The Merry Adventure of the Puppet-Man, with the Memorable Soothsaying of the Prophesying Ape

The little square of the town where Quixote and Sancho rest for the night is galvanized by the arrival of Peter the Puppet-Man, who has a green patch over his left eye and leads a Barbary Ape on a chain.

PETER: Two reales, my masters! Two reales for every one of your questions to which the famous Prophesying Ape whispers the answer in my ear. Two reales!

QUIXOTE: Tell me, Master Peter, fortune teller, what is to become of us all?

PETER: Sir, this animal does not answer or give information about things that are to come and things that are past; he knows something of the present, a little.

SANCHO: Zwounds! I'd not give two beans to know what's past; for who can tell that better than myself? So here's two reales and tell me what my Teresa Panza does now, and in what she busies herself.

PETER: I will not take your money until the Ape has done his duty.

> *Peter gives the Ape its signal. The Ape whispers in his*

> *ear. Peter looks in amazement and then kneels before Quixote.*

Oh, famous reviver of long forgotten Knight Errantry! Oh, never sufficiently extolled Knight Don Quixote de la Mancha! Raiser of the faint-hearted, propper of those that fall, the staff and comfort of the unfortunate! And you, honest Sancho Panza, the best Squire to the best Knight in the world! Rejoice! For your wife Teresa is at this time dressing a pound of flax.

SANCHO: I believe it very well, for she's a good soul.

QUIXOTE: Who in the world could have persuaded me that apes can prophesy? But now I have seen it with my own eyes — for I am the same Don Quixote that this beast speaks of.

> *Applause.*

PETER: Now his power has gone from him, and if you will know any more you must wait till Friday next, when he will answer all you will ask, for his power will not return until then. Yet for the sake of Don Quixote I would forgo all the interest in the world; and to show my duty to him, and give him delight, I will give my puppet show gratis.

> *More applause.*

QUIXOTE: Sancho, I have very well considered this ape's strange quality, and find that this Master Peter the Puppet-man has made a secret compact with the Devil. I wonder very much that the ape has not been examined by the Inquisition.

PETER: Sir: the puppet show is ready, if you will see it.

> *Trumpets and kettledrums. Peter announces each character and what the action of the scene is. The action is mimed to music.*

This true history is taken from the French Chronicles, which are in everybody's mouth, and sung by boys up and down the street. It tells how Don Signor Gayferos rescued his wife Melisendra, that was imprisoned by the Moors in the city of Saragossa.

Our play begins at the court of the Emperor Charlemagne. There, strolling in the courtyard, by the cool of the fountains, is Don Gayferos. "Is not this," he mused, "a blissful place beyond the dreams of ordinary men?"

Take note, good friends, that this once most virtuous knight has fallen into idleness and negligence.

A tall figure calls out from the shadow. "Don Gayferos," he cries. "Unfortunate indeed is the bearer of ill tidings. The virtuous Melisendra, my daughter and your wife, has by the renegade Marsilius been ta'en."

"I know. And care not a jot," replies the indolent knight. "I'd as soon play a game at backgammon than bestir myself for any cause."

On hearing this, Charlemagne — for this is he — strides out from the shadows, his eyes a mighty conflagration. Don Gayferos trembles from head to toe.

Charlemagne is incensed. "This cowardly deed," he cries, "is a stain upon your honour and on mine! Let me rouse your fury!" And with that he gives him half a dozen raps with his sceptre! "Arm yourself! Saddle your proudest steed! Temper your newly found resolve! And ride forth! I have said enough! Look to it!"

"I will, my Lord!" cries Don Gayferos. "Shame me no more! This Marsilius will feel the vengeance of my sword!"

Now turn your eyes to yonder tower. The tower of the Alcazar of Saragossa! The fair Melisendra appears on the battlements.

"Don Gayferos," she moans, "Would that you heard my cry? Better perhaps never to have been born than to submit to the attentions of my Moorish captor."

Will her cry go unanswered?

Quixote is on his feet.

QUIXOTE: I will never, while I live, consent that in my presence such an outrage as this be offered to the fair Melisendra.

Quixote attacks the Puppets.

PETER: Hold! Don Quixote! Hold! Those are not Moors but puppets made of pasteboard.

> *The Ape jumps up and down and then runs away. A sudden exhausted silence.*

QUIXOTE: Had I not been present, what would have become of Don Gayferos and the fair Melisendra? Long live Knight Errantry above all things living in the world!

PETER: Long live in God's name! I am dejected, desolate, poor, and without my ape.

SANCHO: Master Peter: my master is so Catholic a Christian that he will satisfy you with much advantage.

PETER: If he would pay me for some part of the pieces he has spoiled I'd be content.

QUIXOTE: Enchanters put shapes before my eyes, and by and by track and change them at their pleasure. I will pay for all in the current coin of Castile.

> *Quixote pays and goes away. Peter is alone. The Ape peers in and gibbers. Peter signs for it to join him. The Ape does so. Peter lifts up his eye patch and peers around.*

PETER: What they do not know is that I was able to perform that prophesying trick because I am none other than the notorious Ginés de Pasamonte, whom Don Quixote freed with the other galley slaves in Chapter 22 of Volume One. So in the books, as in life, Fortune's wheel is down one minute and up the next!

SCENE FIVE

What Happened to Don Quixote with the Fair Huntress

As Sancho and Quixote ride through a fair meadow they hear hunting music, and then the Duke and Duchess, hawks on their wrists, enter with their Falconers. They see Quixote and Sancho, recognize them, and decide to hail them.

DUCHESS: You: honest Squire!

SANCHO: Me?

DUCHESS: You.

> *Sancho dismounts, approaches, and kneels.*

SANCHO: Lady?

DUCHESS: Rise. The Squire of so renowned a Knight should not kneel. Is not your master he of whom there is a History printed entitled "The Ingenious Gentleman, Don Quixote de la Mancha"?

SANCHO: The very self same, and I am that Squire of his called Sancho Panza.

DUKE: Your master is welcome to our Dukedom.

> *Sancho turns to help Quixote dismount. Between them they get it wrong and Quixote hangs in an undignified upside-down position.*

Ho there! Assist our noble friends!

> *The Falconers help Quixote, who eventually stands before the Duke and Duchess and bows.*

I am very sorry, Sir, that your first fortune on my ground has been so ill.

QUIXOTE: It is impossible, valorous prince, that any fortune should be bad since I have seen you. If my fall had cast me to the very ground abysmal, your glory would have raised me up. So I will always be at the service of you and my lady the Duchess, your worthy lady of beauty, and universal princess of courtesy.

DUKE: Softly, good Sir, for where my lady Dulcinea del Toboso is revered, is there not no reason why other beauties should be praised?

SANCHO: This I say, as a man that has seen many partridges, that my lady the Duchess comes not a whit behind my mistress lady Dulcinea del Toboso.

DUCHESS: Your Sancho is witty and conceited, Sir, and so I confirm him to be discreet.

DUKE: So let us now proceed to my castle, where you shall have the entertainment that is justly due so high a personage, and that we are wont to give to Knights Errant.

SCENE SIX

That Treats of Many and Great Affairs, including the Advice that Don Quixote gave to Sancho Panza

As attendants drape the Duke and Don Quixote in rich cloaks, the scene becomes night in the castle: flambeaux, stately music, and an elegant and courtly dance.

Among the watchers are the Duke's Confessor and the Duke's Steward.

When the dance ends, Sancho speaks to Donna Rodriguez, one of the Ladies-in-waiting.

SANCHO: I pray you, go to the stable, and see that my dappled grey ass is in good spirits.

DONNA RODRIGUEZ: If you are a jester keep your wit until you have use for it — for those that will pay for it.

SANCHO: My master says that in books the waiting women look to the Knight's horses.

DONNA RODRIGUEZ: All I have for you is this fig.

SANCHO: Well: if it's as old as you it's likely to be ripe.

DONNA RODRIGUEZ: Rascal: you stink of garlic.

Everyone has noticed this altercation.

DUCHESS: Donna Rodriguez, with whom are you angry?

DONNA RODRIGUEZ: Here — with this idiot.

QUIXOTE: Sinner: the master is much the more esteemed when his servants are honest and mannerly.

SANCHO: I remembered my Dapple.

QUIXOTE: It would be very fit that your greatness would command this coxcomb to be thrust out.

DUCHESS: Assuredly, Sancho shall not stir a jot from me, for I know he is very discreet.

DUKE: What news, Don Quixote, of the lady Dulcinea? Have you sent her a present lately, any giants or bugbears? You must have overcome many.

QUIXOTE: Sir: when they find her she is enchanted, and turned into a foul creature.

DUKE: Have you seen her enchanted, Sancho?

CONFESSOR: Sir: have I not said many times as your Confessor that it was madness to read of this Don Coxcomb's fopperies? [*to Quixote*] Who, dull-pate, has thrust it into your brain that you're a Knight Errant? Go home in God's name, and look after your stock, and leave your ranging through the world, blowing bubbles and making all that know you laugh. When have there ever been Knights Errant? Where are any giants in Spain? Or bugbears in La Mancha? Or enchanted Dulcineas, with the rest of your troop of simplicities?

QUIXOTE: Is it a vain plot, or time ill spent, to range through the world, not seeking its dainties, but the bitterness of it, whereby good men aspire to the seat of immortality? By my star's inclination I go in the narrow path of Knight Errantry, for whose exercise I despise wealth, but not honour. I am enamoured because there is a necessity Knights Errant should be so, yet I am not one of those vicious amorists, but of your chaste platonics. My intentions always aim at a good end, as, to do good to all men, and hurt to none. If he that understands this, if he that performs it, deserves to be called fool, let your Greatnesses judge, excellent Duke and Duchess.

SANCHO: Speak no more, Master, for there is no more to be said; besides, this gentleman knows not what he says.

CONFESSOR: Are you that fool Sancho Panza, to whom they say your master has promised an island?

SANCHO: I am, and I am he that deserves it. Lean to a good tree and it will shadow you. I have leaned to my master, and if God please he shall not want empires to command, nor I islands to govern.

DUKE: Surely not, friend Sancho. For I in Don Quixote's name will give you an island of mine own.

SANCHO: An island?

QUIXOTE: An island?

DUKE: An island of no small worth.

QUIXOTE: Kneel down, Sancho, and kiss His Excellency's foot.

Sancho kisses the Duke's foot.

CONFESSOR: By my holy order, I am about to say Your Excellency is as mad as one of these sinners. I'll get me home, and save a labour of correcting what I cannot amend.

The Confessor goes. The Duke and Duchess contain their coldly mischievous amusement.

SANCHO: I'll swear that any Knight Errant would have given that gentleman a slash that would have cleaved him from head to foot like a pomegranate.

DUCHESS: To my mind the man is more conceited and madder than his master.

DUKE: Sancho: prepare; put yourself in order to be Governor. For your islanders do as much desire you as showers in May.

Trumpets. Sancho is given a cloak and helmet and his warrant to govern. An anthem is played. The Duke embraces Sancho, and then he and the Duchess leave, followed by their entourage. Sancho and Quixote are alone.

SANCHO: Clad me how they will, I'll still be Sancho Panza.

QUIXOTE: Sancho: although I rejoice for you, your offices and great charges are nothing else but a profound gulf of confusions. So fear God, and consider who you are. Rejoice in the humility of your lineage. Let the tears of the poor find more compassion, but not more justice, than the informations of the rich. Seek as well as discover the truth. When you judge your enemy's case, forget your own injury.

SANCHO: Sir: if you think that I am not fit for this government I will not take it. I had rather be Sancho, and go to heaven, than a Governor and go to hell.

QUIXOTE: Sancho: for those last words I deem you worthy to govern a thousand islands.

They shake hands.

But Sancho: take heed not to belch all the time.

SCENE SEVEN

How Sancho Panza took Possession of his Island

Evening in the town square of Barataria: church bells ringing, cheering crowds. Sancho's procession carries him to the Judgement Seat, where the Duke's Steward bows deeply.

STEWARD: Sir Governor: it is an old custom that he who comes to take possession of this famous island of Barataria must answer to a question that shall be asked him, that must be somewhat hard and intricate, and by his answer the town guesses and takes the pulse of their new Governor's capacity.

SANCHO: On with your question, and I'll answer as well as I can, let the town be sorry or not sorry.

> *A Woman enters, holding on to a man dressed as a Grazier.*

WOMAN: Justice, Lord Governor, justice, and if I have it not on earth I will seek it in heaven! Sweet Governor: this wicked man met me on the highway and has abused my body as if it had been an unwashed rag; and, unhappy that I am, he has taken what I've kept these three and twenty years, defending it from Moors and Christians. I have kept myself as entire as the salamander in the fire and this man must come now with a washed hand and handle me.

SANCHO: This is to be tried yet, whether the gallant's hands be washed or no. What do you answer to this woman's complaint?

GRAZIER: Sir: I am a poor grazier and deal in swine, and this morning I went to sell four hogs. On my way home I met with this woman, and the Devil, the author of all mischief, yoked us together. I gave her sufficient pay but she, not satisfied, laid hold on me, and would not let me go till she had brought me here. She says I forced her, and I swear she lies, and this is true, every jot of it.

SANCHO: Have you any money about you?

GRAZIER: Thirty crowns in silver.

SANCHO: Give it to the plaintiff.

The Grazier gives the Woman the purse.

WOMAN: I pray to God for the Governor's life and health, that is so charitable to poor orphans and maidens.

The Woman starts to go.

SANCHO: Fellow: run after that woman, and take her purse from her whether she will or no, and bring it me hither.

The Grazier goes after the Woman. She stoutly resists, and drags him back to Sancho.

WOMAN: Justice, of God and the World! Look you, Sir Governor. Mark the little shame or fear of this desperate man, that in the midst of a congregation would take away my purse that you commanded him to give me.

SANCHO: Has he got it?

WOMAN: Got it? I'd sooner lose my life than a purse. He'd sooner get my soul out of my flesh.

GRAZIER: She's right. I yield to her. I have no more power. I can't take it away.

SANCHO: Give it to me.

The Woman gives Sancho the purse. Sancho gives it to the Grazier.

Do you hear, sister? If you had showed but half your valour and breath to defend your body that you did your purse, Hercules could not have forced you.

The Woman is very angry.

WOMAN: Hercules? Him? He's a piece of wet string.

SANCHO: Get you gone.

The Woman goes.

In God's name get you home with your money, and if you mean not to lose it, pray have no mind to yoke with anybody.

> *The Grazier bows and goes. The Crowd cheers.*
> *Trumpets.*

STEWARD: His excellency the Governor of Barataria will be served dinner.

> *A table is brought in. There is a Clerk to say grace and a*
> *Page to put a bib under Sancho's chin. Before he has had*
> *one mouthful the plate is whipped away.*

SANCHO: Sir: is this meat to be eaten, or only touched but not swallowed?

STEWARD: It must be eaten, Sir Governor, according to the customs of Governors of islands.

SANCHO: An office that will not afford a man his victuals is not worth two beans.

PAGE: [*to the Clerk*] This town's not an island is it?

CLERK: Of course not — but his Honour's been told it is.

> *A trumpet sounds*

STEWARD: A post from my Lord the Duke, bringing some important dispatch.

> *The Messenger arrives and gives Sancho the envelope.*

SANCHO: Who here is my secretary?

CLERK: I am, Sir.

SANCHO: Let's hear the contents.

> *The Clerk opens the letter and is about to read it when he*
> *checks.*

CLERK: Sir: it is a business to be imparted in private.

STEWARD: What?

> *The Steward snatches the letter and is equally shaken by*
> *its contents.*

SANCHO: Well? What says the Duke?

STEWARD: Turn out the Guard! Guard! Turn out the Guard!

SANCHO: What?

> *Confusion and rushing about. Soldiers start to dress*
> *Sancho in a full suit of armour.*

STEWARD: Arm, arm, Sir Governor. A world of enemies mean to enter the island. They are disguised to kill you, for they stand in awe of your abilities. [*reading*] "Have a care to see who comes to speak unto you, and eat nothing."

SANCHO: Eat nothing?

STEWARD: Arm yourself, or we are undone.

SANCHO: What do I know about arms and succour? I leave those things to my master, Don Quixote. I know nothing of this quick service.

STEWARD: What faintheartedness is this?

CLERK: Arm yourself.

STEWARD: March, Sir. Guard us. Cheer us all. You are our lantern and morning star. March at our head.

SANCHO: How should I march? My knee bones won't move.

CLERK: Bestir yourself. The danger waxes.

SANCHO: Very well. I march.

> *Sancho tries to march but his armour encumbers him and he falls over.*

> *A cabbage is thrown at Sancho. He thinks it is a cannon-ball.*

Oh! I am struck.

> *The others pretend that an attack is in progress. They shout orders, run about, and give Sancho an occasional thwack.*

STEWARD: Victory! Victory! Our foes are vanquished!

CLERK: Sir Governor: rise, rise, enjoy the conquest and divide the spoils!

SANCHO: Raise me. Unbind this armour. I'll divide no spoils but desire some friend, if I have any, to give me a draught of wine.

> *They give him wine.*

What o'clock is it?

CLERK: Sir: it grows to be day.

SANCHO: Give me room, Sirs, and leave to return to my former liberty. I was not born to be a Governor. I would sooner cover myself with a double sheepskin, quickly, than lay me down to the subjection of a government in fine Holland sheets. Every man should exercise the calling to which he was born. Naked I was born, naked I am; I neither win nor lose. So let me go, for it is late.

Sancho's ass Dapple is brought on.

Dapple, when I consorted with you no other cares troubled me. But since I mounted on the towers of ambition four thousand unquietnesses have entered my soul.

STEWARD: We shall be very sorry to lose you, for your judgement and Christian proceedings make us desire your company.

CLERK: What do you need for the journey?

SANCHO: A little barley for Dapple, and half a cheese and a loaf for myself. So I will make my account to the Duke.

STEWARD: You are a grandee, Sancho, and have great reason.

Sancho embraces them, and then leads Dapple away.

SCENE EIGHT

How Don Quixote took his Leave of the Duke

It is a glorious morning. Quixote and Sancho are on the open road, and halt for a moment in the blazing sun.

QUIXOTE: Liberty, Sancho, is one of the most precious gifts that heaven has given men. The treasure that the earth encloses, and the sea hides, cannot be equalled to it. Life ought to be hazarded as well for liberty as a man's honour; and by the contrary, captivity is the greatest evil that can befall man. In the castle, in the midst of those savoury banquets, and those drinks cooled with snow, methought I was straitened with hunger. For I enjoyed nothing with the liberty that I should have done, had it been my own. The obligations of recompensing benefits and favours received are ties that curb a free mind. Happy that man to whom heaven has given a piece of bread without obligation to thank anyone else but heaven alone.

SANCHO: For all that, the Duke did give me two hundred crowns in gold, which I carry as a comforting cordial next to my heart. For we shall not always find castles where we shall be made much of. Sometimes we shall meet with inns, where we shall be cudgelled.

QUIXOTE: Sancho: you are so simple. And I did see Dulcinea enchanted in Montesinos' Cave. I would have you believe it.

SCENE NINE

In which Don Quixote is Feasted in a Pastoral Arcadia

As evening falls a crowd of young people, dressed as Shepherds and Shepherdesses, greet Quixote and Sancho. They are garlanded and romantic and carry musical instruments.

SHEPHERDESS: Sir. Good Sir. Are you not Don Quixote, the valiantest, the most enamoured and courteous gentleman in the world, if your History lies not? And are you not — what d'you call him — Sancho Panza, his Squire, that has no fellow for his mirth?

SANCHO: It's true. I am that merry fellow, and this is the very same Don Quixote aforesaid and historified.

SHEPHERDESS: Stay with us. We are people of quality, and rich.

QUIXOTE: Young shepherds, weary not yourselves, in detaining me, for the precise ties of my profession will let me rest nowhere.

SHEPHERD: We join to make merry in this place; to build a new and pastoral Arcadia with neither sorrow nor melancholy, but in honour of such as your lady Dulcinea del Toboso, that bears the prize for all the beauties in Spain.

QUIXOTE: Since you put it not into controversy we will join you.

> *Quixote and Sancho join the feast by the camp fire.*
> *Sitting near them is a Youth not at all dressed for a*
> *pastoral idyll. His clothes are worn and he has a sword.*

QUIXOTE: You go very naked, Sir, to be one of these gallants.

YOUTH: I am like you, a guest at the fire. Poverty is the cause that
I walk so light.

QUIXOTE: And whither, in God's name?

YOUTH: To the wars.

QUIXOTE: Then the worst that can come to you is death, which if
it be a good death, the best fortune of all is to die.

> *The fire has flickered low. The mood is one of musing on*
> *the edge of sleep.*

Happy times and fortunate ages were those wheron our
ancestors bestowed the title of Golden: not because gold (so
much prized in this our iron age) was gotten in that happy
time without any labour, but because those who lived then
knew not those two words Thine and Mine. In that holy age
all things were in common. No man needed for his
ordinary sustenance to do ought else than lift up his hand,
and take from the strong oak, which did liberally invite
them to gather his sweet and savoury fruit. The clear
fountains and running rivers offered savoury and transparent waters in magnificent abundance. All then was
peace, all amity, and all concord. Shepherdesses went from
valley to valley, and hill to hill, with their hair sometimes
plaited and sometimes dishevelled, with no other clothes
than was requisite to cover that which modesty ever would
have covered. Fraud, deceit and malice had not then
meddled themselves with plainness and truth. Justice was
in her proper terms, for there was neither judge nor
person to be judged. Maidens and honesty wandered, as I
say, where they listed, alone and secure; their loss of
virginity was by their own native desire. But in these our
detestable times no damsel is safe, even hid and shut up in a

new labyrinth like that of Crete, for even there the amorous plague would enter. It was to defend damsels, protect widows and assist orphans and distressed wights that the order of Knighthood was at last instituted. Of this order am I, friend of the wars, and friend shepherds, and I do render you thanks with all my heart.

> *A gentle song. The Shepherds sleep.*

Sancho.

SANCHO: Master?

QUIXOTE: I have a longing upon me to witness that which I have never beheld in all my life.

SANCHO: Master?

QUIXOTE: The sea.

> *Tremendous music crashes forth. The lights change and the stage picture is immediately transformed for the next scene.*

SCENE TEN

Of the Adventure that most Perplexed Don Quixote of any that had hitherto Befallen him

On the sea shore Quixote stares at the breakers.

The Knight of the White Moon enters with his Squire. The Knight, as we shall discover, is Samson Carrasco, completely armoured and visored, and with a white moon painted on his shield. The Squire is Tomas Cecial, with a false nose.

KNIGHT OF THE WHITE MOON: Famous Knight and never sufficiently extolled Don Quixote de la Mancha! I am the Knight of the White Moon, whose renowned deeds perhaps you have heard of. I am come to combat with you, and by force of arms to make you know and confess, that my Mistress, be she whom she will, is without comparison fairer than your Dulcinea del Toboso. Which truth, if you will plainly confess, you will save your life and me the labour of taking it. But if you fight, and I vanquish you, all the satisfaction I will have is that you forsake your arms, and leave seeking adventures, and retire yourself to your home for the space of one whole year, where you shall live, peaceably and quietly, without laying hand to your sword, as befits your estate and also your soul's health. If you vanquish me, my head shall be at your mercy, and the spoils of my horse and armour shall be yours, and the fame of my exploits shall pass from me to you. Consider what is best to be done, and answer me quickly, for I have only this day's respite to dispatch the business.

QUIXOTE: Knight of the White Moon, whose exploits hitherto I have not heard of, I swear you never saw the famous Dulcinea; for if you had, I know you would not have entered into this demand. For the sight of her would have confirmed that there neither has been, nor can be, a beauty to be compared with hers. And therefore, not to say you lie, but that you err in your propositions, I accept your challenge, and at once. I only deny one of your conditions, which is that the fame of your exploits pass to me, for I know not what kind of ones yours be, and am content with my own. Begin your charge when you will, and I will do the like, and so God and St. George!

They take up their stations for the fight.

I commend myself to heaven and my lady!

KNIGHT OF THE WHITE MOON: Blow your trumpets!

A trumpet sounds. Quixote and the Knight charge. Both Rosinante and Quixote are simply bowled over by the Knight's horse. The Knight dismounts and kneels by Quixote.

You are vanquished, Knight, and a dead man, if you confess not according to the conditions of our combat.

QUIXOTE: Dulcinea del Toboso is the fairest woman on earth, and

I the most unfortunate Knight. It is not fit that my weakness defraud this truth. Thrust your lance into me, Knight, and kill me, since you have bereaved me of my honour.

KNIGHT OF THE WHITE MOON: Not so, truly. Let the fame of my lady Dulcinea's beauty live. I am only contented that Don Quixote retire home for a year, or till such time as I please.

QUIXOTE: I will accomplish it, like a true and punctual Knight.

> *The Knight gets up, walks away, and takes off his helmet. Tomas Cecial takes off his false nose. Sancho sees who they are.*

SANCHO: Samson Carrasco? Tomas Cecial? What have you done?

KNIGHT OF THE WHITE MOON: Sancho: take him home.

> *Samson Carrasco and Tomas Cecial go.*

SANCHO: Signor mine, cheer up if you can. Thank heaven that although you came a tumbling cast to the ground, yet you have never a rib broken. Let's home to La Mancha. If you consider it well, I am the greatest loser, though you are in the worse pickle.

QUIXOTE: Peace, Sancho. My retirement shall be but for a year.

SANCHO: She you call up and down fortune is a drunken, longing woman, and withall blind, and so she sees not what she does.

QUIXOTE: Sancho, you are very philosophical, and all I can tell you is that in the world there is no such thing as fortune. Every man is the artificer of his own fortune, which I have been of mine. So in our retiredness we will recover new virtue, to return to the never-forgotten exercise of arms. If you think fit, Sancho, will turn shepherds.

SANCHO: Shepherds? Very suitable to my desire, Sir. I believe the Bachelor Samson and Master Nicholas the Barber will no sooner have seen it than they will turn shepherds too.

QUIXOTE: Now I return, vanquished by the force of a strange arm, and yet at least conqueror of myself. I did my best.

SCENE ELEVEN

How Don Quixote Fell Sick:
Of the Will he made, and of his Death

Quixote comes home to his village.

   The Curate, the Barber and Samson Carrasco are there. Quixote embraces them all. Teresa Panza comes out, and Sancho gives her the gold crowns. The Servant Boy takes Rosinante.

   Finally Quixote is alone with his Niece and Housekeeper.

QUIXOTE: Niece: we shall buy a store of sheep and become shepherds.

HOUSEKEEPER: How can you endure the scorching heat and the cold winter nights? Mind you: if the worst comes to the worst, it's better to be a shepherd than a Knight Errant.

QUIXOTE: Hold your peace.

HOUSEKEEPER: Abide in your house, think on your domestic affairs, confess yourself often, serve God, do good to the poor, and if any harm come to you of it, let me take it upon my soul.

QUIXOTE: Dear good woman: I know what I have to do. In the meanwhile get me to bed. Methinks I am not very well.

> *Music. The Niece and Housekeeper get Quixote to bed. He has a burning fever. They watch as a Doctor feels Quixote's pulse. Night has fallen. Lamplight and shadows.*

HOUSEKEEPER: Be of good cheer, Sir. Be of good cheer.

DOCTOR: The health of his body is in very great danger, through melancholy and troublesome cares.

> *The Niece and Housekeeper fight their tears.*

He must begin to think on the salvation of his soul.

> *The Housekeeper sees the Doctor out. The Niece watches and waits. Quixote seems asleep. Then he awakes.*

QUIXOTE: The Almighty God be for ever blessed, that has done
so much good for me.

NIECE: My Lord and Uncle? Is there some new matter befallen?

QUIXOTE: My good niece, I possess now a free and clear judgement. I feel myself near unto death, but I would not have it
to be such as the surname of fool should rest upon me. For
although I have been foolish in my life I desire not to
confirm the truth of it in my death. Cause my dear friends
to come unto me.

> *They are all waiting outside and the Housekeeper follows
> them in: The Barber, the Curate, Samson Carrasco and
> Sancho.*

My good Sirs: give me some New Year's gift. I am no more
Don Quixote de la Mancha, but rather Alonso Quijana. I
bequeath my property to my niece and acknowledge my
folly. Profane histories of Knight Errantry are hateful to
me.

CURATE: What?

BARBER: It's some new kind of foolishness.

SAMSON: Now that we are so near to become shepherds, will you
become a hermit?

QUIXOTE: Good Sirs: I feel death to follow me at my heels. Let us
leave off merriments and jesting. A man must not make a
jest of his soul. Sancho: my dear friend, pardon me, that I
have given you the occasion to seem a fool, and made you
fall into the same error where I was fallen, that in the world
there have been and still are Knights Errant.

SANCHO: Sir: yield not unto death but endeavour to live many
fair years. The greatest folly that a man can commit in this
world is to give himself over to death without apparent
cause.

QUIXOTE: Go not so fast. In the nests of the last year there are no
birds of this. Once I was a fool but now am wise. All human
things decline from their beginnings until they come to
their last end and period. Yet my end has surprised me,
coming when I least thought of it.

> *Quixote dies. The Curate closes Quixote's eyes. The*
> *mourners pray and the light in the house dwindles, as*
> *Sancho comes down to the audience to speak.*

SANCHO: Here lies the noble fearless Knight
Whose valour rose to such a height;
When death at last did strike him down,
His was the victory and renown.

He reck'd the world of little prize,
He was a bugbear in men's eyes;
But had the fortune, in his age,
To live a fool and die a sage.

> *Tremendous and triumphant music.*

THE END

TWO AWARD-WINNING PLAYS

MARK MEDOFF   *Children of a Lesser God*

Mark Medoff's play examines society's attitudes towards disabled people through two main characters: Sarah Norman, a deaf woman, and James Leeds, a speech therapist who tries to persuade her to learn to speak and lip-read. But it is Sarah who teaches James the beauty and subtlety of her sign-language and shows him that she has a right to an independent existence that defies the norms and expectations of the hearing world.

Winner of The Antoinette Perry (Tony) Award for Best Play of the 1979-1980 Broadway Season and The Society of West End Theatre Awards for The Play of the Year, 1981; Actress of the Year in a New Play (Elizabeth Quinn); Actor of the Year in a New Play (Trevor Eve).

"...a riveting piece of drama...I can't recall any other play that makes it so clear that the so-called handicapped have their own code, their own ethos, their own pride."
Michael Billington, The Guardian

"...a complex and beautiful play..."
Milton Shulman, Standard

NELL DUNN   *Steaming*

Steaming is set in the 'Turkish Room' of a run-down Public Baths in the East End of London, where five women regularly meet to bathe, relax and share their troubles. They are brought into a closer commitment to each other when they organise a campaign to stop the baths from being closed down.

Winner of The Society of West End Theatre Award for The Comedy of the Year, 1981 and The Standard Drama Award for The Most Promising New Playwright, 1981.

"a lovely play suffused with affection"
Ned Chaillet, The Times

"[a] funny and touching play"
Douglas Orgill, Daily Express